The CEO Mechanic

Sandie James

Published by Sandra Hudson

ISBN: 978-0-9944153-3-2
Cover Design by Maryde

DEDICATION

This book is dedicated to my wonderful husband Jim
for
his patience and being my sounding board when
needed.
I love you now and always.
To my children and grandchildren,
Tammy, Colin and Clint
Daniel, Laura, Annabella and Harmony.

You mean the world to me, and bringing me untold
enjoyment and fill my life with love.

CONTENTS

ACKNOWLEDGMENTS

I would like to take this time to thank the wonderful people who have helped me along on my writing journey. To my family for your constant love and support even when I am pulling my hair and ranting about characters not doing what they should. Thank you to Romance Writers of Australia for the ongoing support you give your members. To the Hunter Romance Writers, you girls are the lifeline that keeps me sane.
Thank you to my brothers Len and Robert and my sisters and Lorraine and Sue for believing in me.
Rob thank you for answering my medical questions.
To my beautiful CP's - S.E Gilchrist, Louise Mack and Erin Moria O'Hara thank you
for your honesty and encouragement.
Finally, thank you for the other twelve women who came along on this journey.
It has been a blast working with you all.

***

A Bindarra Creek Romance
Drama, intrigue, suspense, adventure and honest country goodness – welcome to Bindarra Creek where life and love in a small country town has never been more challenging.

CHAPTER ONE

Mac Stafford leaned against the doorframe of the local garage workshop and wiped the oil from his hands on an old rag. In the distance, east of town, a cloud of dust billowed into the air off the gravel road.

The sun was high in the sky and warmed his tanned chest. He had removed his T-shirt while working on a car. The heat inside the workshop was suffocating, even with the door open. The smell of sun-baked earth and grease filled his nostrils.

This end of town was very quiet with only a few businesses in the area. On the opposite side of the street stood Beth's Café—a red-brick building with its red and white awning that covered alfresco-style seating. Beth Roget served the best hamburgers Mac had ever tasted. He could understand why it was a popular stop-over for truckies travelling from the south to Moree.

Further along, the road was Peter's Farm Supplies, where many of the property owners took the time to catch up for a chat.

When he'd first arrived in Bindarra Creek three months earlier, he'd had no idea how long he would stay, but Fred Viders had offered him a job as a mechanic in his garage and Mac decided he had nothing to lose. This small town was as good a place as any to spend his time. Fred was the kind of person you took to straight off the bat, and they'd formed a quick friendship.

The cloud of dust drew closer. Mac put the rag in his back pocket and turned to re-enter the workshop. The Bentley needed a test drive before he could ring the owner.

Mac ran a hand behind the back of his neck to release the growing tension building between his shoulders. *Move, just move and keep busy.* He had tried to leave his guilt behind, but it seemed no matter where he ran, some demons never left him— and his demons ran deep. Idle time was his enemy these days. It was better for him to get back to work. *Keep moving, don't think just work.*

"Hey, Mac." Fred walked around the corner of the white timber building. Of medium height and stocky build, Fred covered his silver-grey hair with an ever-present blue baseball cap.

Mac turned to his boss. "I thought you were going

out of town for a day or two."

Fred handed Mac a cold can of cola. "Here—you need a drink. That workshop is too bloody hot at this time of day."

One thing Mac had learned about Fred very quickly was that he was content to chat more than work. He also changed the topic of conversation if and when it suited him. Mac didn't bring up the question of Fred going out of town again. His friend would tell him if he wanted to.

"Looks like someone is in a bit of a hurry." Fred nodded toward the dust cloud.

"Yeah, I was thinking that myself. They might want to slow down or they could find themselves in some trouble." Mac took a long drink of the cold liquid. It wasn't very often he drank fizzy drinks, but today it hit the spot.

Fred turned to look at Mac. "How's the Bentley coming along?"

"All done, I was just about to take her for a test run then give her a good clean."

"Good, good. Fairfax will be happy, and there's not much that makes that man happy."

Mac glanced over at the road as a Porsche 911 Carrera convertible drove past. He whistled through his teeth admiring the smooth, elegant lines of the vehicle.

"Looks like Brooke's home for the weekend. Haven't seen much of her of late," Fred muttered, more to himself than to Mac. He turned to Mac and said, "Brooke is the youngest daughter of the Fairfax children. She's strong-willed and stubborn as hell like her father, but you couldn't find a friendlier person. Always willing to help those around her. And pretty. One of the town's beauties." Fred smiled and removed his cap to scratch his head. "Wonder what's got a bee in her bonnet today?"

"She doesn't come home much?" Mac asked then kicked himself mentally. *Hell, I don't need to know this.* It was useless information to him. If there was one thing he'd learned over the past few months, it was that you only needed to know what was important to your life, not everyone around you.

"She used to come home most Saturdays to spend time with her mother and young brother, Davey. Louise had a heart bypass a few months back, just after Brooke's grandfather died. Brooke took it damn hard, as you could imagine. She doesn't get on with her father, so Louise has Mathew, their butler run her and Davey into Tamworth on the weekend to have time with Brooke."

"Yes. Well, I'd better get this job finished." Mac turned toward the workshop once again. "Give me half an hour then you can ring Mr Fairfax."

"Right you are. I'll mosey on over to Beth's to see if she knows anything about Brooke's return."

Mac raised a hand in acknowledgement, but made no comment. If Fred didn't know what was going on, Beth would. Beth kept a finger on the pulse of gossip around town. Mac called it the Bindarra Creek

Telegram Association—once one person found out the information, it travelled down the line until the whole town knew what was happening. So, whether he wanted to know or not, Fred would give him the rundown on the youngest Fairfax daughter.

***

On the drive home to Bindarra Creek, Brooke contemplated on what it was she could have done to upset her father this time. She would have ignored his demand to return, except for her mother and Davey.

The thought of Davey brought a smile to her face. He was an affectionate boy and loved being the centre of attention. Her parents had received the news during the pregnancy that Davey had Downs Syndrome. Her father was furious when her mother refused to have an abortion. To this day, he took no interest in his youngest son.

With AC/DC blaring from the speakers, she eased back on the accelerator as she drove toward town, oblivious to the scenery around her. She had driven home enough times to know nothing ever changed. Even though the road hadn't changed much, the council was always doing one thing or another to it. Movement in front of Fred's garage caught her eye as she drove past.

Well, maybe some things do change after all. She peered into her rear-view mirror to get another look at the bare chest of the hunk talking to Fred. *Hmm, I might need to get some fuel later today. There's nothing I like better than a tall, dark and well-toned man.*

She continued through town, took a right on Mt Ingalls Rd and a left onto Wattle Drive. Ruth Edwards, her elderly friend, stood outside watering her garden. Ruth had introduced Brooke to the love of gardening and art. She gave her a toot of the horn and waved. *I'll have to find time for a chat before I head back home.*

Running a hand through her thick hair and pushing it back off her face, Brooke realised it would be a mess by the time she got to the house. Maybe she should have left the car roof up, but the promise of a beautiful day was a temptation she couldn't let pass.

Brooke slowed down then stopped in front of the large bronze gates that barred entry to the Ingalls Estate. It didn't matter that her father had changed the name to Fairfax after her grandpa's death. Brooke would never think of it as anything other than Ingalls Estate.

She pushed the remote and waited for the gates to open. As she drove up the long drive to her childhood home, her stomach lurched at the thought of seeing her father again. From an early age, he'd had this effect on her. It hadn't taken her long to realise she could never measure up to her older siblings.

Oh, won't they take delight in knowing I'm in trouble again. Especially Candice. Yes, Candice would milk this for all it was worth. Anything to make sure she was the one holding up the Fairfax image of elite snobbery. She and Candice had never got along, not even as children.

She drew in a shaky breath and gripped the steering wheel with damp palms. *He can't hurt me. I'm stronger than I used to be*. So why did she feel like she was about to walk through a minefield?

Pulling up in front of the old colonial manor, she took in the grandeur of her ancestral home. She loved the history of her family, the old house and the memories it evoked. Grandpa Henry used to spend hours relaying stories of his grandfather, Elijah, and his father, Albert.

She rubbed at the knot in her chest as she remembered her grandpa. Six months after his death, Brooke still felt the pain of him not being there to welcome her home with his warm, loving smile. A month after his passing, her mother was rushed to hospital with a heart attack and had needed emergency surgery. *Thank God, Mum's progress showed promise of a full recovery.*

The double glass entry doors opened and her father stepped out onto the porch, his hands behind his back. Brooke could imagine him tapping his fingers together, a habit when he grew impatient.

She slid out of her car. "Hello, Father."

Harsh, cold eyes raked her from head to toe as he took in her well-worn jeans, loose T-shirt and sandals. She resisted the urge to tidy her hair. A Fairfax *always* dressed to the high standard expected from one of the town's prominent families.

"Meet me in my study in five minutes, not a

moment later," he replied, an edge of disgust in his tone.

He turned and strode back into the house. His broad shoulders strained against the confines of his grey suit. Brooke couldn't remember a time when she'd seen her father in anything other than a suit. Not even when he sat in the wet bar to relax did he wear anything but business attire. No doubt, many women would say he was handsome, and except for the ever-present scowl, Brooke could admit as much.

She tugged her lower lip between her teeth and smirked. *I wonder if he realises how ridiculous he looks with his hair dyed black. And they say women can be vain.*

Mathew, their butler, came hurrying out the side door as Brooke unloaded her luggage from the car.

"Sorry, Miss Brooke, I should have been here to do that for you."

Brooke smiled at the ageing man dressed in his customary black suit. Mathew had been a tall man when younger, but age had stooped his body and turned his black hair almost entirely grey.

He and his wife Ellen had started work on the estate shortly after her grandparents had married. Brooke loved and respected them like family. Many of her childhood days were spent helping Ellen in the kitchen and learning to cook.

"Hello, Mathew," she said, giving him a hug. She stared into his dark brown eyes, shadowed with darker circles. "I can take this, it's not heavy."

"Now, Miss Brooke, you know your father will not have you carrying your bags when you are here." He reached for her luggage again.

"Oh, poppycock." She waved her hand and moved up the steps with her suitcase and bag in hand. "I do it at home, so I can do it here."

With a warm smile, Mathew held the door open then followed her into the house. She'd no sooner entered than a squeal alerted her to the small boy about to launch himself from the sweeping staircase that descended into the foyer.

"Roo, you here!"

Dropping both her bags on the marble floor, she caught her brother mid-air. She laughed as she held him close and turned in a circle.

Mathew picked up her bags and took them up the stairs to her room.

"Davey, my baby, I've missed you so much." She kissed the blond locks as he laid his head on her shoulder, his chubby arms wrapped around her neck.

"Sweetheart, you have to let Brooke inside before jumping on her." Her mother laughed as she descended the stairs at a slower pace. "Darling, how are you?"

Lowering Davey to the floor beside her and keeping a hand on his shoulder, Brooke hugged her mother close with her other arm.

"Hello, Mum." She leaned back to look at her mother. "You're looking well today."

Her mother looked lovely in a pale blue dress

fitted at the waist, showing her still youthful figure. She carried her age well. No one would ever guess she was in her early fifties. It was the healthiest she'd seen her mother looking since the operation. Her hazel eyes sparkled with affection and her copper red hair sat softly around her oval face.

Her mother returned her hug and kiss. "Thank you, darling. I'm glad someone thinks so."

Brooke cast a curious glance at her mother, but made no comment.

"Come on, buster, Brooke has to speak to your father. You can see her when she's finished," her mother said, extending a hand out to Davey.

"Don't want to." Davey pouted and hugged himself closer to Brooke. "Davey stay with Roo."

Davey always talked about himself in the third person. Brooke found it endearing. She kneeled down beside her brother and ran her hand over his head. "Davey, I need to talk to Father. I won't be long. Then we can have a nice long visit. I'll even read you the new story I brought for you. Okay?"

"Kay." His blue eyes lit with excitement.

Taking their mother's hand, Davey seemed satisfied knowing he would be getting a story read to him soon.

"Do you know why I've been summoned, Mum?"

"No, darling, I didn't even know you were coming until an hour ago."

Her mother's eyes carried a hint of sadness for a moment then it disappeared. Her parents' marriage had not been a happy one for many years, and Brooke often wondered why her mother tolerated her father's affairs and arrogant manner.

"He did mention something about having a dinner party tonight. He has poor Ellen, Mathew and Jillian running around like chooks with their heads cut off." Louise sighed.

Davey burst into tears.

Brooke knelt once more by her brother. "What's up, sweetheart?"

"Davey doesn't want chooks with no heads," he sobbed.

"Oh, sweetheart, Mummy didn't mean the chooks had their heads cut off ..."

"*Brooke*!" A tight roar came from her father's study.

"Crap," she muttered and gave her brother's hand a squeeze.

Her mother would explain to Davey what she meant. Right now, Brooke needed to get this interview out of the way.

The study was located off the timber-panelled hall. He would have heard her talking to her mother and Davey, and that would have only made him angrier. Putting anyone before the mighty Gordon Fairfax was a misdemeanour punishable by a good tongue-lashing.

When she was younger, the lashing had at times been physical, until Grandpa found out and threatened to have her father kicked out, not only from the house, but also from Ingalls Development. Her father couldn't argue as Grandpa still had control over all the finances and the family business, which Henry Ingalls had built up from the ground. Ingalls Development had an office in Tamworth as well as the original office in Bindarra Creek.

Her father had taken over Grandpa's study two years ago when Grandpa had decided to slow down and step back from the family business. The room had undergone a complete redecoration after Grandpa's death to fit with her father's personality. The once warm room now held an air of intimidation.

Composing herself, she squared her shoulders and walked into the study. The strong smell of tobacco hung in the air. Gordon's only weakness was a good cigar, and he enjoyed nothing more after a day's work than to lean back in his leather chair with a brandy and a Cuban. He ruled the rest of his life with unflinching dominance. Brooke shuddered at the thought of both.

The room was very masculine with its timbered walls and ceiling. Dark, heavy drapes hung on either side of the double glass doors. The thick cream carpet was the only thing that broke the darkness of the room. The Fairfax family crest, which Brooke was sure her father had designed, took pride of place behind his desk. Photos of her father with politicians, judges and other noteworthy people hung on the walls though. There were no family photos anywhere. This room belonged to her father now, his domain, and it was his accomplishments which were placed on display.

Brooke slouched into the black leather seat in front of her father's desk waiting for the hammer to fall. She didn't have to wait long.

Her father slapped the morning newspaper on the desk and pointed to the front-page article. "I see you found yourself in a bit of a scrape last night."

"I wouldn't call it a scrape. I'd call it more of a right to choose who puts his hand up my dress." *If he wants a reason to come down heavy, he can look elsewhere.*

The picture showed her kneeing a guy in the crotch. The photo of the man who'd harassed her, taken the night before, looked like it may have come from CCTV footage. No doubt, her father would have had one of his spies following her too.

Brooke lifted the paper to read the article that accompanied the photo. The headline read, *Local Artist in Nightclub Skirmish.*

Local artist and daughter of property developer Gordon Fairfax, Brooke Fairfax, was caught last night in a skirmish with an unknown man. It is believed that Ms Fairfax had been out with friends when she was approached by the man who made an unsavoury comment. Bystanders said Ms Fairfax asked the man politely to leave. When he refused and made a grab for her, Ms Fairfax kneed him in the region of his groin. The man was escorted from the premises.

"So you go out, pick up some pervert, then change

your mind when he makes a pass at you?"

"Father, I have no idea where you get your information from, but I didn't pick up some random guy." She gritted her teeth.

Why does he always assume I'm in the wrong?

She stood, ready to leave then leaned over his desk instead and looked him straight in the eyes. "I was having a drink with friends. This creep kept butting in. I asked him nicely to mind his own business. He took offence at being brushed off, so he put his hand up my dress and told me he could show me a good time. I kicked him where it hurts. If that's leading a guy on, you need to get your spies to watch things more closely. I take it you didn't bother to read the article? If you had, you would know what really happened."

She turned to walk to the door, her heart hammering against her chest. *Hell, he is the limit.*

"Where the hell do you think you're going?" he roared.

Hand on the doorknob, she turned and said, "Out to see Mum and Davey. Then I'm going home. The smell in this place makes me sick." She opened the door.

Her father rounded the desk faster than she thought he was capable of. He grabbed her arm in a vice-like grip and loomed over her, his dark eyes burning into hers. Her heart pounded in her chest.

He won't hit me, I'm older now. He won't hit me.

"You will go nowhere until I am finished with

you."

"Why? What more is there to say?" She clenched her teeth and counted to ten under her breath. "Tell your people to be a bit more vigilant when summing up a situation." She would have to make things up to Davey on their next visit.

Her father slammed the door shut and pushed her back towards the chair. "Sit down. There is another matter I wish to discuss with you."

Staring at him, she braced her hands on the back of the chair. "I'm not interested. I just want to see Mum and Davey then go home."

"Sit!"

Brooke did as her father said and slumped against the back of the chair. Her father was a man not to cross.

He took his seat behind the desk. "I will speak to my person."

And that folks is as close to an apology as I'm going to get.

"I'm having a dinner reception tonight."

"Yeah, so Mum said." She shrugged. "Sorry, I didn't bring any evening clothes with me."

"Yes, I knew that would be the case, which is why I had Rosemary pick up a dress and shoes from town for you to wear. Everything you'll need will be laid out in your room."

Rosemary Watson had been her father's personal assistant for five years. Brooke was sure the woman would like to be more, but not even Gordon Fairfax would carry on an affair under his wife's roof.

"What if I don't want to go?"

"You will be there, Brooke," he ordered. He leaned back against his chair and rubbed a finger across his lips. "If not, David may have to miss out on his next visit with you. Your mother has things to occupy her here."

She narrowed her eyes. *Oh, he's good. He's very good.* He knew how much the weekly visits meant, not only to her, but also to her mother and brother. They'd spend the day shopping, go to the movies or hang around her studio, painting.

Recently she'd started a painting of her mother and Davey which she hoped to have finished for her mother's birthday in a month's time.

If not for them, she would not let him have this control over her. *I couldn't bear not being able to see either of them.*

"Fine, but don't expect too much from me." She stood and left the room, closing the door behind her.

She leaned back against the wall outside the study and drew in a few deep breaths. Tears stung her eyes.

This is stupid, he can't hurt me anymore. It's not as if I've ever been important to him.

***

"Mac, you around?" Fred called from the front of the workshop.

"Yep, out back. What's up?" Mac had been cleaning up the area, ready for Monday. He was methodical like that in everything he did. He liked a clean space to start out in each day.

"I need you to take the Bentley out to Fairfax. He says he's too busy to come and pick it up. He'll have the cheque ready when you get there."

Mac sauntered to the front of the shop. Amused, he said, "And why do I have to do this?"

"Because I hate driving, you know that. And I'm just as likely to put a dent in the bloody thing."

Mac had realised early in their acquaintance that Fred was not much of a driver. If they went anywhere, he always threw the keys to Mac.

"Okay, give me fifteen minutes to clean up and I'll be on my way."

He took the steps at the side of the garage two at a time to the small flat above the workshop. Fred had told him he could use the rooms above the garage until he found something more permanent. Mac had yet to tell Fred he was happy with the arrangement as it was, and he wasn't even looking for another place.

Opening the front door, he stepped into a good-sized kitchen and living area. It was scantily furnished with sofas, a coffee table and a small television, plus an old timber dining table and four chairs, but it worked well for Mac.

The apartment was neat and tidy now that he'd cleaned it up and made it liveable for humans. He smirked as he recalled his first sight of the living quarters. Fred's idea of only needing a little cleaning had taken Mac two weekends before he could move in completely.

There were two bedrooms at the back of the flat which overlooked the main road. One Mac had turned into a small office with his laptop, an old desk he had picked up at a garage sale and a fold-out sofa. The only thing he'd spent any real money on was his bed.

The old bed in the main room had almost done his back in that first night. Luckily he was able to pick up a bed and some linen the next day and have it delivered that afternoon. He'd moved the old bed to the shed out the back. No one should have to suffer that sort of torture.

Mac had a quick shower and dressed in clean jeans and T-shirt. He grabbed an apple out of the fridge, remembering he'd missed lunch.

Fred waited for him at the front of the workshop. "Now be careful with this baby, Mac." Fred looked slightly flushed. "I don't want Fairfax to have any reason to complain. Mathew, their butler, will bring you back to town."

Giving the older man a light slap on the shoulder, he said, "It'll be safe with me, mate. Just tell me where I have to go."

"Oh, right." Fred removed his cap and scratched his head for a moment, a sure sign the man was flustered. "Go through town. Main Road runs onto River Drive, the estate is on the right. You can't miss it. The old fart has Fairfax written on the bloody gate, for heaven's sake. Not that it was always Fairfax Estate. Used to belong to Fairfax's wife, Louise's family, but when Henry Ingalls died six months ago, Gordon apparently believed he'd earned the right to change the name. Mind you, people around here still call it Ingalls Estate."

Mac was still laughing as he pulled out of the garage. He liked his employer and had taken Fred into his confidence regarding the circumstances that had led him to the town. He didn't need the money he earned, so he donated it anonymously to Pastor Miller's Church renovations.

Driving up Main Street, Mac noticed Florence Miller, the pastor's wife, and president of the local CWA at the helm of the Friday cake stall. Pamela Brown, head of the Bindarra Creek Telegram group, and Beatrix Fukuka were once again on duty with Florrie.

Reaching the Fairfax Estate, Mac pushed the button on the intercom system to announce who he was, stated his business and waited for the main gate to open. He'd often passed this way when he'd been out for a ride on his Harley, but had never taken much notice of the estate.

The bronze gates were impressive even by Mac's standard, with Fairfax Estate inscribed on them. A black metal security fence ran around the perimeter of the property. Gates open, he drove up to the front of the house. The lawns were manicured, the garden beds well-tended. Two decorative fountains stood on either side of the drive. French doors opened out onto the porch of the impressive sandstone home.

Out front stood the blue Porsche that had sped past the garage earlier in the day.

Climbing out of the car, Mac headed over to get a better look at the Porsche. It was a 1975 model and in excellent condition. *Brooke Fairfax knows her cars.*

He turned toward the front door as a lean, elderly man dressed in a black suit with coat tails called him over to where he stood near the side gate.

"Sorry, sir, but only family and friends use the front entrance."

Mac didn't comment. What could he say? He was here as the hired help, so to speak.

"I'm Mac." He held his hand out to the older man.

"Nice to meet you, Mac. Mathew is my name." The butler gestured to the side of the house. "Come in. I won't be a minute. I'll just take Miss Brooke and Master Davey their refreshments."

Mac followed Mathew into a large open-plan kitchen. It was a hive of activity, people moving about everywhere. Worried he'd get in the way, Mac stayed close to the back door. Mathew picked up the tray from the bench and motioned Mac to follow him.

What's going on here? It's like a bloody top class restaurant.

A large island bench stood in the middle of the room, surrounded by three young people dressed in white jackets, black and white checked pants and black hats. An older girl dressed the same, but wearing a white chef's hat, explained to them how to decorate some form of dessert. A woman with a pleasant face gave instructions to two girls working at an industrial-sized stove.

"Miss Brooke is out on the garden patio. We can go via the garage to the estate car."

Mac dodged across the room, trying to avoid crashing into anyone. Mathew moved as if there were no one else around but him. They walked out to a sunken porch of slate tiles filled with tropical plants in large ceramic pots. Shells decorated white tables while on one wall hung paintings of bright tropical scenes.

A large window provided a view of the garden filled with native Australian plants. The whole effect gave the room a lived-in feel, Mac thought. So unlike his own family home with its sterile environment.

At one end of a large floral sofa sat a young woman with her arms wrapped around a young boy, reading him a story. Her hair fell over her shoulder in a mass of coppery red curls. Her voice changed as she read a new character in the story. They were so engrossed in their story time, neither noticed others had invaded their solitude.

Mathew placed the tray on the table in the middle of the room. "Refreshments, Miss Brooke and Master Davey."

So this was Brooke Fairfax. *Nice ... very nice.*

She lifted her head and smiled, until she saw Mac standing behind Mathew.

"I'll be running Mac home now, Miss Brooke, and then I'll start on the other jobs that need attending to before tonight."

She removed her arms from around the young boy and stood with all the elegance of a ballerina then strolled towards them. There was something in the way she carried herself. Not portentous, only natural grace. Her grin brought her face alive. She was stunning before she smiled, but now she was downright gorgeous. Straight white teeth behind lush full lips, and a light sprinkling of freckles dusted across her delicate nose. However, it was her eyes that drew him in. Jade green rimmed with thick dark lashes lured him into the depths of her very essence.

Mac's pulse raised a notch or two. *I could find myself in trouble with this one. Just as well, I'm only the hired help.*

"Hello, I'm Brooke Fairfax," she said, holding out her hand. Her voice was as pure as freshly gathered honey. "And you are?"

"Mac, Miss Fairfax." He accepted the small fine-boned hand she offered him.

"Brooke." Those eyes sparkled with mischief. "Mac? No other name?" She arched a perfect brow.

"No." He shrugged. "Just Mac."

The young boy of no more than six bounced up to them, a ready smile on his oval face.

"Davey, this is Just Mac. Just Mac, this is Davey." Brooke introduced them.

Davey laughed, a laugh so hearty Mac couldn't help but join in. Mathew stood beside Davey with an affectionate gleam in his eyes.

"Juzz Mac, Juzz Mac," Davey sang, delighted he had the attention of all three adults.

Mac hunched down so he was level with the boy and shook Davey's small hand. "It's nice to meet you, Davey." Like his sister, he had a dusting of freckles across his nose.

"Me Davey, you Juzz Mac." The boy gave him a toothless smile. "Roo read Davey a dragon story." He made a growling sound.

"Is that so?" Mac looked up at the woman before him. "And does the knight slay the dragon?"

"Oh no, this is a good dragon, isn't it, Davey?" Brooke ruffled the boy's hair.

"Yeah, good dragon." Davey twisted his arms together and swung his body back and forth.

"What the hell is going on in here?" A bellow came from behind them.

Mac straightened.

"Nothing, Father. We were meeting Mac."

"No, Juzz Mac," Davey insisted.

Brooke smiled at the young boy beside her while Gordon Fairfax scowled. Davey took a step back to hide behind his sister.

Mac frowned. Fairfax was a big man, not just in stature, but in height. He stood a good two inches taller than Mac.

"Sorry, Mr Fairfax, it was my fault," Mathew volunteered. "I was giving Miss Brooke and Master Davey their refreshments before taking Mac back to town."

"So you're the young whippersnapper from the garage." Gordon Fairfax stared down his distinctive nose.

It had been a long time since Mac had been called a whippersnapper. Prudently, he hid his amusement. "Yes, sir." He held out his hand, but the gesture was ignored.

"Hmm ... Mathew, run him back to town then get to the rest of your chores. You have the cheque for that old fool?"

"Yes, Mr Fairfax." Mathew retrieved it from his inside pocket and handed it to Mac.

Mac's amusement vanished at hearing Fred being call an old fool. *Opinionated air bag.* He couldn't put his finger on it, but something in Fairfax's demeanour triggered wariness in Mac. He thought he was pretty good at assessing people, and Gordon Fairfax spelled trouble.

"I'll take him back," Brooke piped up. "Mathew has more than enough to do. Davey and I would love to go for a drive. Wouldn't we, Davey?"

The young boy began to jump. "Yes, take Juzz Mac home."

Fairfax glared at them all for a moment before turning to leave. "Do whatever you want. Just make sure you're back in time to get ready for tonight. I want to give Stafford a good impression, so don't be late, girlie."

Not hearing Brooke's reply, Mac stared as Fairfax left the room. Stafford? His mind raced at the thought that his father could be coming to town. *What are the odds that Fairfax is talking about Dad?*

Of course, he could be wrong, but he'd learned to trust his gut. And what if he was right?

CHAPTER TWO

Brooke led Mac through a door at one end of the patio to where she had parked her car earlier. "Davey, you jump in your seat, please."

"Davey not want to." The young boy pouted.

"It's okay, I can sit in the back."

Brooke's gaze ran over his tall frame and she smiled. As much as she'd like to see him try to squeeze that magnificent body into the small space, she knew she couldn't do it to him.

"No, Davey has to learn he has to obey the law and sit in his child restraint seat. Davey, if you're good I'll get you a surprise, okay?"

She sent Mac a wink, knowing this would do the trick with her brother. As long as he thought he would get something in return for his good behaviour, he'd be happy. For now, she wanted to have time to get to know this hunk of a man.

"Kay."

Davey crawled into his seat, and Brooke leaned in to buckle up his seatbelt before hopping in behind the steering wheel. Watching Mac squeeze his large frame into the passenger seat was like savouring your favourite sweet.

He looked just as good up close as he did from a distance. Shame he was wearing a T-shirt now. His thick dark hair was dishevelled as though he spent a lot of time running his fingers through it.

I'd like to run my fingers through that hair.

His navy-blue eyes were highlighted with specks of grey, and a sexy five o'clock shadow emphasised his bronzed tan. His presence seemed to take up the whole car. His fresh, woody aroma caused a little tingle to flutter in her belly. For someone who worked as a mechanic, he smelled fresh. Not that she knew what mechanics were supposed to smell like. She'd never had much to do with them other than dropping her car off for a service.

Brooke was disappointed when he pulled his sunglasses down over his eyes. Putting the car into gear, she negotiated her way down the drive. The gates opened with the press of a button on her remote.

"So, how long have you been in town?" she asked, hoping to find out more about him.

"Not long, about three months."

"Are you enjoying yourself?"

"Pretty much."

"Tell me a bit about yourself," she pushed. She had to find a way to get more than a few short sentences out of him.

He shrugged his wide shoulders. "Not much to tell, I'm Mac ..."

"Juzz Mac." A small voice came from the back.

"Yes, Just Mac." He laughed.

He had a great laugh. It sounded like it started in his belly and worked its way up past his chest. She'd like to start at his belly and work her way up. Who was she kidding? She'd like to start lower and work her way up, and then go back down again. Her attraction was strong, and she wasn't sure she liked it.

Why this guy? She hadn't had a reaction like this since Wilson. *And look where that got me.*

"I'm a mechanic who works for Fred."

So deep in thought, Brooke was thrown when Mac spoke. *That's what happens when your mind wanders to things you have no right thinking about with Davey in the car.*

"What about you?" he asked.

"Me? I don't have much of a story. I'm the youngest daughter, rebellious—or so my father will tell you. I'm an artist earning her way in the world."

"So you don't take handouts from Daddy?"

Was that sarcasm in his voice? She spared him a glance. "No, I haven't for a long time. I've been lucky with a few private commissions and a couple of showings at galleries in Sydney. I'm quite happy to be independent of my father."

"Is that luck or hard work?"

"A bit of both, I guess," she replied, somewhat startled. Not many people thought of her art as hard work. *A point in his favour.*

"This is an impressive car and well looked after," he commented.

"Thanks, I bought it last year. It's beautiful to drive." She ran her hands lovingly over the black steering wheel. It had been her reward after selling her first lot of paintings.

"So what's with the party tonight?"

"Who knows?" She sighed. "My father wants to impress some guy and have him believe this would be a great place for a new development, but I have a feeling there's more to it." She shrugged. "I'm not consulted in the running of the family business." *Although, that's about to change.* "I just hope Mr Stafford knows his business."

"Any reason Stafford should be worried?"

"Nothing I can put my finger on. Why the interest?"

"No reason, just small talk. Would you mind stopping at the CWA cake stall?"

Brooke smirked. "Sure."

She negotiated a parking spot in front of the IGA store where the cake stall was set up.

"I won't be long."

Brooke was impressed at how easy Mac unfolded himself from the car. It also gave her a good view of his scrumptious behind.

"Davey want cake please, Roo."

"Okay, why not, but you have to keep it for after your dinner." Brooke helped her brother from the car and walked over to where Mac stood talking to Florence Miller.

"Now, Florrie, you know if I take another cake I'll have to run an extra ten kilometres tomorrow," he was saying as she reached his side.

Florrie? It seemed Mac was well entrenched in the community if he was calling Mrs Miller Florrie. She smiled at the pastor's wife.

"Hello, Mrs Miller."

"Brooke dear, how wonderful to see you home," said Mrs Miller. From the glances she was giving Brooke and Mac, she no doubt thought she had a new lead on some town gossip.

"It's lovely to be home," Brooke lied. "Davey would like a cupcake, if he may."

There were cakes and slices of all kinds displayed on one table with another filled with craft items from knitted babywear to toilet roll covers. Brooke remembered her mother telling her once that most of the women involved with the CWA were wonderful knitters.

Mrs Miller looked down at Davey. "Have you been a good boy today, Davey?"

She earned herself a toothless grin. "Davey always

good. Roo said."

The adults laughed.

"Well, in that case, you can have your pick of the cakes."

Davey's face lit up with delight at the selection of superhero cakes. In the end, he selected one decorated with a Superman topper.

Brooke glanced at the two elderly women at the back of the stall and recognised them as the sisters who'd lived in Bindarra Creek for as long as she could remember. "Hello, Mrs Brown, Miss Collins."

"Oh, it's Mrs Fukuka now, dear," the quieter of two sisters replied with a blush.

"Well, congratulations."

"She married a Jap," Mrs Brown threw over her shoulder from where she was collecting more cakes to place on the table.

Brooke widened her eyes in surprise. Mrs Brown had always been direct, but that was a bit *too* direct.

"Pamela, really!" Mrs Miller admonished. "Can you not show some respect for your dear brother-in-law?" She turned to look at Brooke with an assuring smile. "Makishi is a real gentleman, and so kind."

From the corner of her eye, Brooke noticed Mac leaning so his hip rested on the table, arms folded across his magnificent chest. He tucked his sunglasses into the top of his T-shirt.

Mrs Brown placed a selection of slices on the table. "Florrie, you know as well as anyone Makishi is a Jap."

Mrs Miller rolled her eyes. "You could at least call him Japanese."

Brooke watched the interplay between the women with amazement. She noted the new Mrs Fukuka stood in the background with an almost serene smile on her lips.

Brooke gave herself a mental shake. *Lord, let's not even consider what she might be thinking.*

Davey tugged at her hand, reminding her of his presence.

"Sorry, darling, we'll go soon."

"My treat," Mac said when Brooke went to pay.

Mrs Miller stared at them again in that peculiar way she looked when she was plotting something. "So, have you two been dating long?"

Brooke choked back a laugh when Mac's features went from amused to dismay.

"Oh, we're not dating, Florrie. We've only just met," said Mac, the tips of his ears turning pink.

A man who blushes, I'll be.

"Well, you make a lovely couple. Perhaps you should think about it." She smiled. It was clear she had matchmaking on her mind. "Now, here you go, Mac. I hope the banana cake is up to our normal high standard."

"Yes, you do make a lovely couple," Mrs Fukuka put forward.

"Oh, for heaven's sake, Beatrix, just because you've found love after all these years doesn't mean every man and his dog is looking for it," her sister inserted.

"How's Jonas going these days? I haven't seen him around for a while," Mac asked.

Brooke got the feeling Mac was aiming to divert another round of words between Mrs Fukuka and Mrs Brown.

"Oh, he's busy with the church renovations." Mrs Miller clasped her hands in front of her as if offering up a prayer. "Some kind soul has been leaving money in our letter box with a note telling him to use it for the Church. They left fifteen hundred dollars just this morning," she whispered.

Mac whistled through his teeth. "That will come in handy."

"Yes, it's like the good Lord has answered our prayers." Her eyes shone with excitement.

"Well, I'm glad Jonas can work on the Church."

He handed the woman a twenty-dollar note. "Keep the change."

"You are a sweet boy, Mac."

Mrs Miller was right. Mac was one very sweet boy. *Good thing I have a sweet tooth.*

Brooke noted the warmth in his eyes as he turned to Mrs Brown. "Pamela, do you have my special order?"

"Oh, yes. We only made it yesterday so you may want to let it settle for a while." She pulled out a bottle of wine from under the table. Mac handed over a fifty-dollar note and waved his hand when Mrs Brown went to give him change.

"Is that ...?" Brooke began only to see Mrs Brown

touch the side of her nose with her forefinger. *Could this scene get any weirder?*

After encouraging Davey to say goodbye, Brooke took his hand and they walked back to her car.

"You're very generous with the ladies," she said as she buckled Davey into his seat.

"There's only me and I get free rent so ..." Mac shrugged.

"Do you even drink that strawberry wine?"

He glanced over at her with a twinkle in his eyes and said no more.

"Where are you staying?" she asked as they hopped back into the car.

"In the apartment above the garage." He leaned his arm on the door and glanced at her with those intense blue eyes before dropping his sunglasses back into place.

The heat of a blush coursed over her skin. *Lord, it's hot in this car.* She resisted the urge to fan herself.

"Davey wants ice cream, please."

"Maybe after we drop Mac off," Brooke told him.

"Juzz Mac," Davey corrected.

"Looks like you have a new name."

"Yeah." His smile rocked her to her toes.

"Juzz Mac come too." Everything Davey said was more a polite order, not a question.

"Davey, Just Mac might have things to do."

"No, I can come for ice cream," Mac said.

Brooke shivered as his deep baritone washed over her like warm chocolate on a cold winter's day.

"Oh okay, we'll go to Beth's."

A few minutes later, she pulled into a parking spot out the front of the old café and truck stop.

"I've got this," Mac said.

Slightly amazed, Brooke watched as Mac helped Davey from his seat, collected his cake and bottle of wine before taking Davey's hand and leading him into the café. The low rumble of his voice filtered back to her as he spoke to Davey while they found a table.

He really is an unusual man.

The dimple in his cheek when he smiled all but melted her bones and had her wanting to jump his, but there was more than just the superficial aspects of him. From all she'd seen in the last half hour, he was a good man. His generosity to CWA was not just monetary, he showed genuine interest in the women behind it, but his patience with Davey surprised her, treating her young brother as an equal. He had the ability to look past Davey's disability and see a normal loving child, and it touched her heart.

Brooke shook her head. *If I'm not careful, I'll start believing in love at first sight.*

A lot had changed in Beth's café since she'd had taken over the business ten years before. Brooke and her friends used to come in for a milkshake and chips after school, and play the jukebox that still stood in the corner. The once torn seats in the booths that lined two walls of the room were now reupholstered in deep crimson material. The greasy walls were now clean and covered with posters of old advertisements for drinks and food. And it was a thriving business.

Beth, a petite woman in her fifties, walked over in six-inch platform shoes. A pink uniform showed off her slender figure and stretched across her substantial breasts while her shoulder-length, platinum-blonde hair looked to be teased within an inch of its life. A broad smile spread across her heavily made-up face when she recognised them.

"Well, this is a pleasure, Mac. Not like you to turn up at this time of day."

"Davey would like an ice cream, and I thought I'd enjoy one as well," Mac replied.

Brooke grinned when Beth glanced over at her brother and winked. "Well, Mr Davey, what sort of ice cream can I offer you today?"

"Strawberry, please."

"Now I wonder why I'm not surprised." Beth gave a throaty laugh.

It was one of their rituals to come into Beth's for an ice cream before going out to Bellevue Stables for a ride when Brooke came to town. Davey enjoyed giving the old pony he rode carrots or an apple.

I'll have to make time to do that while I'm here. It's been too long since we did that last.

"It's lovely to see you home, Brooke." Beth gave her an inquisitive stare.

Brooke laughed. "I take it you saw this morning's paper?"

Beth had the good grace to blush. "Yes, well you can't help but see. It's front page news! I take it you had a rough night."

Brooke noticed Mac following the conversation with interest. "I was in a bit of an altercation last night, one of the reasons I'm home today."

"Davey want ice cream, please."

"Sorry, sweetheart, I'll get that for you now. What about you?" She glanced at Mac and Brooke. "Ice creams or a drink?"

"I'll have a strawberry ice cream as well thanks, Beth," Mac said.

Brooke smiled. "Make that three, please."

As Beth walked away to get their order, Mac glanced over at her and raised an eyebrow. And what an eyebrow it was. *Lord, he's gorgeous.*

"Do you get into altercations often?"

Brooke picked up a paper napkin from the table and started to shred it. "Not as much as I once did. I outgrew trying to upset my father for the fun of it." She smiled over at him.

He gave her a slow sensual smile that made her want to climb over the table between them and devour those wonderful lips. His gaze dropped to her mouth then up again. Heat flared in his eyes.

She let out a long sigh. *Thank God, I'm not the only one feeling the attraction.*

Pulling herself back from her wayward thoughts, she said, "It doesn't take much on my part to set my father off, I just have to look the wrong way and he flies into a rage." She shrugged. "Meanwhile, my older siblings pander to his every need, and I swear they take great delight in seeing me in trouble. That is the sadistic element of my family. So playing happy families at the dinner party should prove an interesting evening." She gave a shallow laugh. "I know it makes me sound very petty." *Why am I telling him all this? I hardly know the guy.* She frowned.

Mac reached over and rubbed his thumb over her knuckles where her hands rested on the torn napkin on the table. "No, it doesn't, I get the feeling you'd like to have harmony within your family. We all crave that. Don't be so hard on yourself."

Beth arrived with their ice creams.

Embarrassed and confused, she slipped her hand out from under his and made sure the rest of the conversation centred on Davey—like how much he loved his ice cream, even if most of it was on his face.

They said their goodbye out the front of Beth's.

"Where Juzz Mac go, Roo?" Davey asked.

Brooke ran a hand over Davey's hair. "Home, baby. He lives across the road in that building."

As Brooke watched Mac cross the road, a shiver ran down her spine. *I should keep my distance from the hunky mechanic, he's far too unsettling for my peace of mind.*

***

Mac jogged over to his flat after saying his farewells to Brooke and Davey. He'd ring Alice, his personal assistant, and get the lay of the land for tonight's dinner.

Besides, that would keep his mind off the delectable Brooke Fairfax. Just thinking about her sent his system into overdrive. He'd never reacted to a woman with this sort of intensity before, and he was not at all happy about the situation. Not one little bit.

He pulled his mobile from his jeans pocket as he opened the door to his flat, and searched for Alice's number. Mac switched on the coffee pot then leaned back against the cupboard, waiting for an answer.

"Mac! It's about time you called. Your dad is worried sick about you," Alice reproached him.

"It's only been a fortnight since I last spoke to you." Mac rolled his eyes.

Alice Monroe was in her late forties and extremely efficient. Even though she was only ten years older than him, she treated him like a son, never short of giving him a dressing down if she thought he needed it. Alice was an integral part of Stafford and Sons, and if he didn't love her like a sister, he'd have fired her years ago.

"I can't help but worry about Roland, Mac. He's looking tired."

A stab of guilt hit his heart at the mention of his father. "I'll be home soon, I promise. Why I rang ... is Dad going to a dinner tonight?"

He made his coffee as Alice gave him a rundown on what she knew about the dinner and the proposal Fairfax had presented to Stafford and Sons Development.

"Thanks, Alice. I'll give Dad a call now. That might help settle him down."

"You should have done that before now, my boy." She hung up before he could answer.

Of course, Alice was right. There was no real reason he couldn't ring his father other than he didn't want to talk about Garry.

Guilt hit him again when he acknowledged the steps he'd taken to stop his father from contacting him. He'd bought a new mobile phone and left his old one at his apartment in Sydney. Berating himself, he ran a hand across the back of his neck and dialled his father's mobile.

"Dad, it's me."

"Son, where are you? How are you?" his father asked, thickly.

Mac swallowed. "I'm okay. I just needed some time alone."

"Son, when you told me you were taking off for a while, I thought you meant for a week. It's been almost three months now."

Placing his mug on the coffee table, he dropped onto the sofa and ran a hand through his hair.

"Dad, I know and I'm sorry, but I'll talk to you about that later, I promise. What I want to talk to you about now is the new development. I have concerns about this Fairfax guy. I want you to promise me you'll be on your toes with him."

"Son, you're talking to your old man here. I ran this business for years on my own. Is that where you're staying? Bindarra Creek?" The hopeful tone of his father's voice caused another spasm of guilt to rush through Mac's body.

Mac ignored the question of his whereabouts.

"I know how business savvy you are, Dad, but I think we should have the team do a more in-depth investigation into this guy's background."

His father was right, of course. Stafford and Sons had a crack team when it came to any new venture they were interested in backing, but his gut told him this would not be a normal business association.

And that, damn it, is what concerns me.

"Don't you go worrying about me, son. What I want to know is when you're coming home?"

Squeezing his eyes shut, Mac fought the well of grief bearing down on his chest. *Damn.* Voice rough, he said, "Soon, Dad. I still need some time to get my head around Garry's death."

Mac heard his father's intake of breath. He knew this wasn't easy for the old man, but the fact that Mac and his stepmother, Maureen, had done nothing but fight since Garry's death was not healthy for anyone. Especially his father.

"Son, Garrison's death wasn't your fault."

"Yeah, well you tell Maureen that."

"Okay, Brit, I get your point."

His father had always called him by his middle name, Brit, for as long as Mac could remember. The guilt rolled over him again. His father would be battling his grief. *Have I taken the easy way out?* But

Mac needed this time away to come to terms with the fact that he hadn't been there when Garry needed him most.

"I have to go, son. Maureen is finally ready."

"Where are you?" His stepmother hated not being able to stay in the swankiest hotels. Bindarra Creek's motel was in no way up to Maureen's standards.

"We're staying in a villa just outside of Armidale. We'll make the dinner on time. Still have an hour up our sleeves."

Mac's gut contracted. After this preliminary meeting with Fairfax, Steve Zenox, one of their top development managers, would be the one doing all the follow-up meetings. He thought if he could avoid seeing Maureen, he wouldn't mind catching up with his father.

"I'll talk to you again soon. I love you, Dad."

Mac disconnected before he could hear his father's response. It had been a long time since he'd told his father he loved him. It wasn't something fathers and sons did, but he'd felt his father needed to hear it tonight. He headed to his bedroom, dropped onto his bed and laid back, staring up at the ceiling.

He'd blocked the last conversation he'd had with his brother from his mind on purpose. He didn't want to remember. The call informing him of his brother's death had been one of the most horrific of his life.

Mac rubbed his hands over his face, surprised to find it damp. Tears for the brother he'd lost. He sat up and began to pace the room. The arguments with his stepmother had followed, her face contorted with hate.

"This is entirely your fault. If you'd been there for him, if you'd taken the time to talk to him, my baby would still be alive. You were always jealous of Garry. I knew you wanted him dead, you all but murdered my son…"

The ever-present nightmares of his brother's death plagued his sleep and threatened to consume his soul.

Rehashing this stuff wasn't doing him any good. He needed to get out for a while. He grabbed the keys to his Harley and went downstairs. A ride out on the open road was what he needed.

CHAPTER THREE

Brooke stared critically at herself in the Cheval mirror that stood in the corner of her bedroom. The floor-length red evening gown with its deep plunging neckline, open back and shoestring straps revealed the unicorn tattoo on her shoulder. The split that opened to the top of her right thigh made her cringe. She supposed she was lucky she could at least wear a g-string under the thing.

She ran a hand over her upswept hair, making sure every strand was in place. Soft curls framed her face and she was happy with the effect she'd achieved. Her makeup was minimal, merely lipstick and mascara. The only jewellery she wore was three gold bracelets and her watch. She knew the moment she walked downstairs, her father and older siblings would criticize her.

Brooke had sat with Davey while he ate his dinner then taken him up for his bath. Zara, his nanny, was under strict instructions that Davey was to stay in his room, or her job would be on the line. She didn't like Zara's chances. If there was one thing Davey hated, it was losing his chance to be the centre of attention. Their sister, Candice, entered through the front door as Brooke descended the stairs.

"Brooke darling, Daddy told me you were here."

"Candy, sweetheart." She battered her eyelashes. "Here I am, summoned to the Big House under orders to behave."

"Yes, well, we all know how hard that is for you to do."

Candice, as always, had her straight blonde hair pulled back in a tight bun. The effect made her sister's features hard. Brooke had always thought Candice would be striking if she relaxed a little and did away with the intense business dress code she favoured. Even now, she wore a dark blue suit. It wasn't that the outfit didn't flatter Candice's slender figure, it nipped in at the waist and sat neatly on her hips. The skirt reached to her knees showing shapely calves. Stiletto shoes added to her height.

She could feel Candice's critical eyes on her as she walked into the dining room to see if she could help.

An expensive white linen cloth covered the long dining room table. Only the best for her father. Three silver candelabras, each holding five long candles, was positioned down the centre of the table. Brooke fiddled with the cutlery on the table to make sure it was all placed just so or her father would have a fit and some poor soul would suffer.

"Brooke! Really," her sister hissed. "We have staff to do that."

Brooke glanced over her shoulder at her sister before turning back to check the table.

"How many are coming tonight?" she asked.

"It's just a small gathering of twelve. The mayor and his wife, of course, along with Councilman Towns—Daddy's hoping to take over his seat in the next council election—and his lady friend, Mrs Reynolds. Plus Rosemary to even up the numbers. Daddy didn't want too many. The more here, the less time he'll get with Mr Stafford. After all, Stafford is the big fish tonight."

When Brooke finished with the table, she turned to find her sister watching her.

She leaned against the back of a chair and folded her arms. "Do you have a problem, Candy?"

"I would prefer if you call me Candice."

"What? I've always called you Candy," she said innocently, knowing it upset her sister no end.

"I think it would be best if you stay away from Mr Stafford," Candice told her.

Brooke arched an eyebrow. "Why am I here if I'm not to talk to him?"

"Daddy wants us *all* here. So you are to be seen, but not heard."

Brooke lifted her hand and gave her sister a salute. "Yes, madam. No problem, madam."

"You are such a smart bitch at times."

"Brooke, are you upsetting your sister again?" Her father strutted into the room, adjusting his jacket as if he was just about to receive some great award. Dressed in a black tuxedo with a pristine white shirt and black bowtie, Brooke had to admit that her father looked every inch the successful businessman. *Too bad that success was on Grandpa's coat tails.*

"I thought that was why I was here, to get under Candy's skin." She gave them her sweetest smile.

"Watch your mouth, girlie, no wonder you find yourself in so much trouble all the time." His lips pinched.

She received the same lecture every visit. She wasn't good enough, she had a smart mouth, *yadda yadda yadda...*

"Well, I'll leave you so Candy can kiss your arse some more."

Her father's face flushed red and his nostrils flared. Brooke walked out of the room with her head high, but tears stung at the back of her eyes. She went into her grandpa's suite at the back of the house to compose herself.

Why do I care? I don't need father's approval nor do I want it. I never have, so why is it bothering me now? Grandpa, please help me get through tonight.

A spine-chilling scream rose from beyond the dining room. Her shoulders tightened. *Davey.* She hurried into the dining room as fast as she could in six-inch heels. Zara held Davey by his wrist, twisting his arm trying to drag him to his feet. Davey cried uncontrollably, fighting to get away from the despicable woman.

She scowled at her father and sister. "Let him go, *now!*"

On shaking legs, Brooke raced over and picked her young brother up off the floor. He wrapped his arms around her neck and his legs around her waist. She pressed her lips onto the top of his head.

"Roo," Davey sobbed, "Davey ... want Mummy."

Her father stood sipping a scotch, talking to Candice as if Davey wasn't even there.

"It's okay, baby," she soothed before turning on her father and sister. "What is wrong with the two of you?"

"The child needs to learn obedience. A little discipline won't hurt him," her father said in a clipped voice.

"Discipline? There is a big difference between discipline and abuse," Brooke snapped.

"Oh for heaven's sake, Brooke," her sister hissed at her. "Take the little re—"

Brooke glared at her sister then pinched Candice's upper arm as she walked passed.

"Crap, Brooke you'll bruise me."

"I'll do more than bloody bruise you if you ever call Davey that filthy word again," she said through gritted teeth, then flung her sister's arm away from her.

Brooke carried a shaking Davey upstairs to his room. He wept into her shoulder. Zara trailed slowly behind them. *I'll see that woman gone by the end of the weekend.*

She settled him on his bed and kissed his forehead. "Go to sleep now, Davey."

He said sleepily, "Davey want to see Juzz Mac, Roo." He rubbed his eyes with his fist.

Sitting on the bed beside her brother, Brooke brushed a lock of hair from his forehead. "Sweetheart, Mac is busy tonight. Maybe tomorrow we can go and visit Just Mac. Okay?"

He nodded and rolled over onto his side with one hand tucked under his cheek and the other holding onto a ragged old teddy Brooke had given him for his first birthday. "Kay."

"I love you, little man." She stood, ran her hand through his blond locks and said goodnight.

Zara was in the adjoining room folding some of Davey's clothes and packing them away. With clenched fists, Brooke stalked over to the nanny.

"If I have my way, this will be your last night here, so start looking for a new position," she said in a controlled tone.

"With all due respect, Miss Brooke, it isn't any of your business." The woman glared smugly at her for a moment before turning back to her chore.

"Don't push me, Zara, or you'll be gone tonight," Brooke warned.

Shaking with anger Brooke left the room to see her mother hurrying along the hall towards her, fear etched in her green eyes, her face pale.

Her mother looked every bit the elegant hostess in a white evening gown with a black lace overdress that fell gracefully into a fishtail skirt.

"Darling, is he okay?" her mother said in an anguished whisper.

"He's very upset, Mum. He was asking for you." Brooke rubbed a finger to her temple. "I've given Zara a warning about hurting him."

Her mother's hand went to her throat. "Zara hurt him? Oh, Brooke," she choked. "She is so good with him when I'm around them."

Brooke gathered her mother into her arms and rubbed her back. *Lord, having to worry about Davey isn't something Mum needs now.*

"Mum, I wonder if it might be best to have Zara dismissed."

Her mother nodded her agreement. "I never wanted a nanny in the first place, but your father was most insistent after my illness. Do you think there's a chance she has done this before?" Tears glistened on her mother's lashes.

"I don't know, Mum. However, we shouldn't take this lightly. Maybe it would be best to have someone come up and stay with Davey as well."

"Yes, yes, you're right. I'll go and give him a kiss goodnight." She covered her mouth with a trembling hand. "We can ask Ellen if she can spare someone to sit with him."

Brooke slumped against the wall clutching her hands to her chest while she waited for her mother to return. *Has Father condoned Zara's punishment of Davey before now?*

"He's sleeping now," her mother said, coming out of the room. "Zara wasn't in the room. Hopefully, he'll sleep through the night, but I'll come up later to check on him."

"Okay, Mum." Brooke held her mother's arm as they descended the stairs.

"It's about bloody time you got yourself down here, Louise," her father growled as they stepped into the sitting room. He flung his arm towards the kitchen from where he stood near the drinks cart. "Go and make sure everything is in place and make bloody sure the staff knows what I expect of them."

"Father, I'm sure everything is under control," Brooke replied.

Why can't he see the strain in Mum's face after the incident with Davey? Is he that cold-blooded?

"Did I ask you?" He glared at her with eyes filled with ice. "Candice is right, I should never have called you home."

"Great, I can get changed and sit with Davey."

"You'll do no such thing. The table's set." He waved a hand in the air. "Go with your mother. The two of you are exactly alike."

"Gordon, please," her mother said.

"Why thank you, Father. I think that is the nicest

thing you've ever said to me." Brooke smiled sweetly at her father.

Turning, Brooke slipped her hand through her mother's arm as they walked away. Her father's rants followed them to the kitchen.

"You really shouldn't upset your father that way, Brooke," Louise said, sighing.

"Poppycock, Mum. He did nothing to protect Davey tonight, just stood there drinking his damn scotch."

Her mother patted her hand. "We'll get it sorted tomorrow."

They entered the kitchen which was a hive of activity with Ellen in the middle of it all, making sure everything ran smoothly. Brooke walked over and wrapped her arms around the housekeeper's waist from behind her.

"You love this, don't you, Ellen?" she asked. "So many people to boss."

Ellen slapped her hand good-naturedly. "You cheeky little minx, you only come now to give me a hug?" she said in her heavy Italian voice.

"Sorry, I let other things get in my way." Brooke planted a kiss on her cheek and walked over to the bench.

"Is everything under control, Ellen?" Louise asked, gazing around the room.

"Yes, all is on schedule. Mathew has three young men organised to wait on the table and serve the appetizers."

There were never any problems with Ellen and Mathew in charge of things. She saw her mother give their housekeeper a pleasant smile.

"Can you spare Jillian to go and sit with Davey for a while?" her mother asked.

"Is the nanny not well also?" Ellen asked, obviously concerned. "I've had to send one of the girls home. She was feeling unwell. I have no one I can spare for about an hour."

Her mother waved her hand. "Don't worry, it should be okay."

"We had better go, Mum. The guests will be arriving soon." Brooke snuck an appetizer from one of the trays and laughed as Ellen smacked her hand.

Placing her hand over her stomach, Brooke followed her mother from the kitchen. Social gatherings like this were not her style. Not anymore. Now she preferred more intimate dinners. Just a few of her close friends sitting around enjoying each other's company.

By the time they walked out to the sitting room, her brother Duncan had arrived. Brooke closed her eyes. *Now Duncan will be putting his two-bob worth in along with Father and Candice.*

"I see the black sheep of the family is here for the evening." His voice held the same vindictive tone he always used when he addressed Brooke. Duncan was the younger version of their father, not just in the way he dressed, but also his manner. His dark hair brushed back from his high forehead, he gulped down the remains of the dark liquid in his glass.

"Duncan, I see you brought your drinking hand with you."

She wrinkled her nose. Duncan was known to like his alcohol. He was never in the house more than two minutes before he had a tumbler of whisky in his hand. From his bloodshot eyes, Brooke would guess that either he'd started drinking very early or he had a hit-up before he arrived. More than likely he'd had both.

"Okay, I'll have no more bickering. We are to show we are a loving family, united in our goal to develop an estate," Gordon said, thumping his glass onto the cart.

Brooke snickered. "Father, you have got to be joking. Us? United? That's a stretch of the imagination."

"I want this deal, girlie. Stafford is big on family loyalties. He's just lost his son, so now is a good time to approach him. He won't be thinking too much of business."

"Have you stooped so low that you would take advantage of a man when he is mourning the loss of his son?" Brooke asked and turned to her mother. "Do we have to be part of—?"

"Remember what I told you earlier, girlie," her father boomed.

The doorbell rang before her mother could answer. Within minutes, Mathew was announcing the guests and showing them into the sitting room.

Mayor Barry Donaldson and his wife, Gloria, were the first to arrive. Barry wore a dark blue dinner suit that strained against his large stomach, and his stringy brown hair was combed over to hide his bald spot.

Gloria's stylish purple evening gown with a split up to her thigh hugged her body. Her dark hair and tan-colouring showed her Filipino heritage. Rosemary followed slowly behind, dressed in a strapless silver gown.

Waiters walked amongst the guests offering champagne, soft drink and appetizers. The other couple was Councilman Roy Towns and his friend, Heather Reynolds, who wore a charming three-quarter length teal gown.

"Mr and Mrs Stafford, sir," Mathew announced fifteen minutes later.

Mrs Stafford was quite stunning in a white figure-hugging, floor-length gown with a knee-high slit and beaded halter neckline. Her dark hair was pulled back into a braided bun. Like her father, Mr Stafford wore a black tuxedo.

Brooke watched on, amused as her father fawned over Mr and Mrs Stafford. He placed himself between the guests of the hour. Mrs Stafford's hand was placed on her father's arm as she spoke to him. Mr Stafford had turned to speak to her mother.

Introductions were made between the Staffords and other guests. Brooke remained in the background as instructed, watching the interplay between the couples.

Her gaze fell on her mother. Mr Stafford seemed to be taking an interest in what her mother was saying. They both looked her way then strolled in her direction. She smoothed her hand over her dress and shot a quick glance towards her father and siblings. The forced smile on her father's face did nothing to hide the anger in his eyes. *Obviously, Mum hasn't been told to keep Mr Stafford away from me.*

Mrs Stafford had almost plastered herself to her father. One hand rested on the back of his neck as she whispered in his ear. It was quite comical to see her father in this situation. He didn't know whether to follow her mother and Mr Stafford or continue talking to Mrs Stafford. Seeing their intimacy, Brooke wondered if they knew each other before tonight.

"Darling, Roland wanted to meet you." Her mother beamed. "He has one of your paintings in his office."

"I picked it up from an exhibition last year. A wonderful abstract."

Brooke stared at the man in surprise. "Not many people know who I am." She laughed. "Nor are they interested in my abstract paintings."

Roland Stafford was a handsome man with striking blue eyes over a straight nose and warm, full lips. He's grey hair was clipped short with a parting on the left side.

"My dear, I find your art very intriguing. You capture light and texture in your work very well."

"Thank you, Mr Stafford."

Rupert Skinner, a friend and art gallery owner,

had insisted on showing some of her work in Sydney last year, but while she had received encouraging reviews for her landscape and portrait work, her abstract works had received only lukewarm reactions.

"Call me Roland. Now what I want to know is how many more pieces you have finished."

Brooke laughed again, drawing everyone's attention to them. "I have a few, but Rupert has the best of them at his new gallery in Armidale."

"Well, at some time I would like to commission you to paint something for me."

"That would be an honour, Roland," she replied breathlessly.

She wanted to jump and hug the man. *My first abstract commission.*

A short time later, Mathew announced dinner. Roland sat next to her mother, placed at the end of the table, with Candice on his right. Brooke, seated opposite, watched as Candice tried to draw Roland into conversation about the new estate proposal their father had planned.

Roland patted her sister's hand. "My dear, I'm sure this is all very interesting, but I don't talk business when I'm eating. Not while I'm in the company of such lovely ladies."

Candice gave an impression of a fish gulping for air. She glanced down to their father. His pinched lips said it all. He was not impressed that Candice was unable to draw Roland into a business conversation.

"This is an excellent wine," Roland commented, holding his glass up to the light.

"It's from our local winery, Storey Family Wines," her mother responded warmly. "I like to purchase as much of the local produce as possible."

"Very commendable." Roland nodded his agreement.

They had just finished the third course when Zara ran into the room, her face flushed. "He's gone, Mrs Fairfax."

Brooke jumped up at once, knocking her chair to the floor. Her mother followed, jerking to her feet.

"Zara? What's the matter?" Brooke asked, her shoulders tight.

"One minute he was in his bed and the next he was gone." The words tumbled from the nanny's mouth.

"What do you mean *gone*? Have you checked the house?" Louise asked her face pale and stricken.

"No, I came straight down here." The woman turned to Brooke. "I thought he might have come looking for you again, Miss Brooke."

Maybe he's in his favourite hiding place. Davey always hid in Brooke's room when they played hide and seek. Brooke called out to Mathew as she hurried towards the foyer. Her father's voice stopped her mid-stride.

"Louise, Brooke, leave it to the staff."

Brooke turned towards her father.

"He will come out when he gets hungry." He waved his large hand in the air. It was as if his son being missing was of no importance.

"Sir, with all due respect, Davey kept saying he wanted to see someone called Juzz Mac," Zara said in a rush. "I had no idea what he was talking about."

Mac? Brooke shot her mother a frightened glance. Knowing Davey and how determined he was when he had his mind set on something, he could be anywhere on the road. Out in the paddocks. Near the river. *Heavens!*

Brooke grabbed her mother's cold hand. "Zara, when did you last check on him?"

The nanny looked away and Brooke's heart sank.

"Just after you put him to bed, Miss Brooke. Your brother called out saying he wanted to see this Juzz Mac person. I told him he was very naughty and to go to sleep."

Brooke glanced at her watch. "That was a good two hours ago!" she shrieked. "What the hell have you been doing?"

Brooke felt a hand on her back. She looked up to see Roland standing beside her and her mother. Her father continued to eat as he talked to Mrs Stafford. *Are they both that cold? Didn't they care that a small child could be lost outside?*

"Who is this Juzz Mac person?" Roland asked.

"Oh, he works in town as a mechanic. We met him today and Davey took a liking to him." Brooke rubbed a finger over her forehead.

"Mrs Fairfax? What would you like us to do?" Mathew asked.

Most of the other guests had stood to see what they could do to help.

"Err ... Mathew, take some of the men and search the grounds," her mother's voice broke as she spoke.

"Mum, I'll ring Mac at the garage and ask for his help, then drive into town. Hopefully, I'll find him along the way."

"All right, dear." Her mother's voice was hardly above a whisper, her hands visibly shaking.

Candice came to their mother's side and said, "I'll search the house with the staff from top to bottom. Mum, you stay with me."

Thank God for Candice. Mum does not need this added stress, not after earlier tonight.

"We can take my car. I'll drive while you look out for your brother," Roland offered.

"I'll ring as soon as we find him," Brooke said, squeezing her mother's trembling hands.

"Maureen, get up and help Louise look for this boy," Roland snapped.

Lips pinched tight, Maureen Stafford didn't look pleased at having her *tete a tete* interrupted. Nevertheless, she rose to help with the search. Brooke didn't even bother looking to see what her father and brother were doing.

"Do you wish for me to call the SES, Brooke?" Barry Donaldson asked.

"Thank you, Mayor, but I think we'll check for ourselves first." Brooke didn't want to think that Davey could be somewhere where only the SES might be able to search. Somewhere like the river.

Sitting in the front passenger seat of the Stafford's car, Brooke rubbed her hands in her lap. The gates to the estate stood open. With no barrier to keep him in, Davey would have walked straight out.

"I'm sure your little brother will be fine, Brooke," Roland said. "Have you rung that man yet?" He stopped at the entry of the drive.

"Oh heavens, no," Brooke said, pulling her mobile phone out of the pocket of her jacket. She checked her contact list until she came to Fred's number for the garage. It rang twice.

"Fred's garage."

"Mac! It's Brooke Fairfax, sorry to ring you like this." Her tone sounded high-pitched, even to herself.

"Brooke?" His rich-timbered voice came down the line. "I thought you were having a dinner party."

"I was ... Mac, its Davey," she choked. "I think Davey is walking to your place."

"My place? But why? Never mind that. I'll go down and see if I can find him."

"Mac, I'm on my way to town now. Mr Stafford is driving me into Bindarra Creek now. Davey left home anywhere up to two hours ago."

Mac was silent for a moment before he responded. "Hell, Brooke he could be anywhere. I'll grab my bike, search the outer streets of the town, and get Fred and Beth to do the main road. If you and Mr Stafford drive along River Road, that will have the town covered. You'd best give me your mobile number."

She rattled off her number. "Thanks, Mac. I'm sorry for all this trouble."

"It's no trouble. I'll see you soon. Bye." He hung up before Brooke could say anything more.

"Mac suggested we look along River Road. He and some friends will do the interior of the town. If you turn right here, it will take us along the river."

Roland nodded and turned onto the road. Brooke gazed out the window, hoping she would see her brother walking by the side of the street. Her anxiety grew with each passing minute. *Davey could be anywhere. What if he isn't walking along the side of the road? What if he's fallen somewhere*? They could have passed him and not even realised it. She glanced over at the river. A cold shiver ran down her spine. She dragged in a deep, rasping breath.

Roland reached over and squeezed her hand. "We'll find him, I'm sure we will."

Brooke gave him a strained smile then turned back to look out the window.

***

Mac snatched the keys to his bike off the kitchen table and raced down the stairs two at a time, pulling on his jacket as he went. It wasn't a cold night, but with Davey wandering around in the night air, he'd need something warm to put around him when they found him.

He rode onto the main road from the side entrance of the garage and headed over to Beth's. The few streetlights this far from the centre of town only gave a little light.

His mind raced at a hundred miles an hour as he pulled up in front of Beth's and killed the engine, leaping from his bike.

"Beth!" he shouted as he headed for the café.

Beth came outside, followed closely by Fred.

"Mac, what in heaven's name is wrong?" she asked.

"Young Davey Fairfax has gone missing. Brooke seems to think he's on his way to find me for some reason."

"Oh my heavens, that poor little tyke." Beth placed a hand on her chest and turned towards her café. "I'll just let Betsy know that Fred and I will be needed for the search. There are a few truckies just finishing dinner, I'll ask them to help too. You go on ahead of us, Mac, we won't be long."

Beth and Fred were both members of the local SES team, and if nothing else she knew how to organise a search party.

Mac lifted his hand in acknowledgement. "I'm going to do the inner streets if you guys can do the main road."

"Right you are." Fred scratched his head.

Mac started his bike then headed up Main Street before taking a left at Court Street then a right onto Willow Tree Avenue, standing up over the seat of his bike, scanning each side of the road. "Blast."

He turned left at Main Street again before taking the next left onto Banksia Drive and did the same thing. He repeated the process on Wattle Drive. He narrowed his eyes when a small form lying in front of the fire station caught his attention. Turning off his bike, he kicked the stand into place and ran over to the small body.

Davey lay on his side with his hands tucked under his cheek. Mac bent down to make sure he was okay. His pulse was strong, but he was cold. After shrugging off his jacket, Mac lifted the boy into his arms.

"Davey, can you wake up for me, buddy?" He wrapped his jacket around his body.

Davey opened his eyes and his face broke into a triumphant smile.

"Juzz Mac!" he shouted. "You find Davey."

Davey wiggled his arms out of the jacket and wrapped them around Mac's neck.

Mac held him close to his body and laughed. "Yes, I did find you."

He pulled his phone from his pocket and dialed Brooke's number.

"Hello?"

"I have him. We're at the fire station."

"Oh, Mac, thank you! We're just around the corner." Her voice quivered.

A few seconds later, a car drew to the curb. Brooke had the door open even before the vehicle stopped.

"Davey!" Tears ran down her face as she took her brother in her arms "Oh, Davey, I was so worried about you."

Now Mac was faced with the problem of his father.

Mac hoped his dad wouldn't say anything that would give away his identity in front of Brooke. Why that was important he didn't know.

His father stepped out of the car. The incredulous gaze on his father's face was easily discernible even in the dim light. Mac shook his head once, hoping he would get the message. Then he glanced down at Brooke and Davey, amazed to see that they both stood in the circle of his arms. Brooke reached up and kissed him, her lips warm against his cheek.

I wasn't expecting that.

"Thank you, Mac."

She sounded shy, for a moment almost breathless, and then turned her attention to her young brother.

"Juzz Mac," Davey said sleepily.

Mac cleared his throat. "No problem."

Fred's battered old truck stopped on the opposite side of the road. Beth rushed to the front of the truck. "Oh my, praise the Lord," she exclaimed, putting her hands to her mouth.

Mac dropped his arms from around Brooke and Davey.

"I'll ... um ... just ring Mum," Brooke said.

Extending his hand as he walked over to his father, he said, "Thank you for helping Brooke."

His father shook Mac's hand. "It was my pleasure. She is a wonderful girl."

Mac looked back over his shoulder to where Brooke stood talking to Fred and Beth.

"Yes, she is," Mac replied. And for a moment, his

pulse quickened.

He turned to stare back at his father, who was watching him with concern in his blue eyes. Guilt washed over Mac as he noticed how tired and stressed his father looked.

"Dad, we'll talk later, I promise. For now, let's get Brooke and Davey home."

"I won't wait long, son."

Mac returned to the small crowd gathering around Brooke and Davey with his father close behind. It seemed the whole café had come out to help with the search. He shot a quick glance at his father. Mac wasn't someone who showed his weaknesses, especially to his father, but he was starting to realise he couldn't hide forever.

CHAPTER FOUR

The chill of the night was setting in as Brooke sat in the back seat of Roland's car with Davey resting on her trembling knees. The lack of sleep was starting to show as Davey bartered to get his way. Her mother had said she would ring Doctor Warner to come out and check Davey to make sure there were no ill effects from his adventure.

"Davey not want to go." He pouted.

Normally Brooke could make her brother come round to her way of thinking, but tonight he refused.

"Davey, honey, we have to go home. Mummy is worried about you."

He huddled himself into Mac's jacket, wrapping the oversized article around his body. Brooke was thankful for the added warmth for her brother.

Mac knelt down beside the young boy. "Davey, your mum wants to see you're okay. Wouldn't you like to go home?"

When Davey looked solemnly back at Mac, Brooke knew he saw the man as his hero. "Davey want Juzz Mac." He slipped a hand out from the jacket and wiped the tears away with his fist. "Mummy come to Juzz Mac's."

Brooke's heart squeezed tight as she glanced from man to boy. It normally took Davey a while to warm to strangers, but with Mac he had bonded instantly. Her mother had been beside herself with anxiety when they spoke. She needed to get Davey home as soon as possible.

"Well, how about I come home with you?" Mac asked. "I can follow you home on my bike."

"Davey come with Juzz Mac." Davey was nodding in agreement even as he offered a compromise.

"Why don't we all go together," Brooke said. They had to get a move on before her mother became too worried. "That is, if you don't mind, Roland."

"Not at all," Roland agreed.

"I can run you back later," she told Mac. *Hell, what is the matter with me? This man is trouble of the capital T kind.*

It was too late. Davey was scrambling off her lap to sit beside her and started to bounce up and down with excitement that Mac was coming home with them.

"Juzz Mac, sit with Davey, please," her brother

piped up.

"I wouldn't want to interrupt your parents' dinner party."

"Too late, it's already interrupted."

Her father would not be pleased that his evening had been disrupted, his plans tossed out the window.

Although, if he wanted to impress Roland, he'd do well to show some compassion towards Davey, but I won't hold my breath.

***

"I'll ride your bike back to the garage, Mac," Fred said.

Mac glanced at his friend. "You don't like driving."

"That's true." Fred nodded. "But I like riding bikes. Use to be a cross country rider in my day. I've been waiting to get on this beauty since you rode into town."

Unsure if he trusted Fred with his bike, he stared at Brooke and Davey for a moment, but found little option other than to go with Fred's suggestion.

"All right, but be careful, it's a lot heavier than other road bikes."

His father touched his arm. "We'd better go."

Mac slipped into the back seat next to Davey, and the boy snuggled close.

The front doors stood open as they hurried from the car and up the steps, Davey's head resting on Mac's shoulder, the boy's shallow breathing indicating he'd fallen asleep. Mrs Fairfax stood illuminated by the light from the doorway, her hands clasped before her.

His father said something about leaving, but Mac didn't take much notice.

Brooke's mother's hand brushed gently across sleeping Davey's brow. Her pale cheeks wet with tears.

"We'll take him upstairs," Brooke told him over one shoulder before wrapping an arm around her mother's waist.

Mac's mouth went dry as he followed Brooke up the stairs to Davey's room. She'd handed her coat to Mathew as they walked in the door, revealing a smooth white back, a blue and gold unicorn tattoo on her right shoulder blade. It had to be the second sexiest thing he'd seen that night. That dress was made for removing very slowly. He dragged his eyes away before he had a major physical reaction that would really embarrass him.

"Davey's room is this way," Brooke said.

"Looks like you could do with laying down yourself, princess." He had no idea why he called her that except that it sounded right.

"No, I'm fine." She rubbed her temple with a finger. "Mum, I think we should get Doctor Warner to check you over when he finishes with Davey."

"No, let's just concentrate on Davey," Mrs Fairfax replied in a whisper.

Mac lowered Davey onto the Thomas the Tank Engine bed. A raggedy teddy lay at the foot. The room was painted in a light blue, with posters of Disney characters arranged on the walls. A portrait of Davey sitting and playing with his toys hung above his bed.

As he straightened, he noticed tears in Brooke's eyes. He reached for her chilled hand. Mrs Fairfax sat on the bed with her son.

A tall, fair-haired woman stood quietly fidgeting in the background. Brooke's eyes opened wide as if surprised to see her there.

"Candice."

The other woman hesitated for a moment before replying. "I ... um ... was waiting with Mum and wanted to make sure Davey was all right." It was almost like she was embarrassed to admit she cared.

"I wouldn't have managed without Candice." Mrs Fairfax gave her older daughter a frail smile.

"Sorry," Brooke said. "Mac, this is my sister, Candice."

"Thank you so much for your help, Mac," she said, without moving from where she stood.

"It was no trouble. I'm just glad we found him safe."

***

"Where's Zara?" Brooke frowned as she glanced around the room.

"I sent her to bed once we knew Davey was safe," her mother replied tightly. "She was making things worse with her babbling."

Silence fell on the room as they waited for Doc Warner. Brooke wrapped her arms around her body, fighting to stop herself from shaking. A strong arm circled her waist, tucking her in close to a warm, hard chest.

"He'll be all right, princess," Mac whispered against her ear.

She turned in his arms, resting her cheek on his shoulder. Tears burned at the back of her eyes. She snaked her arms around him. It felt good to have someone hold her.

"Doctor Warner is here, Mrs Fairfax," Mathew said from the door.

Peter Warner had been their family doctor since he opened his practice as a young man. Now his hair was greying and he wore it a little longer than most men his age. Brooke thought it was because he no longer had his wife to remind him he needed it cut. Mrs Warner had passed away only a month ago from a heart attack, and it was evident the toll was heavy on the man.

Doc Warner's wire-rimmed glasses sat precariously on his overlarge nose. He walked over to the bed, his limp more predominant than usual.

"Thank you for coming, Peter," her mother said with a hitch in her voice. She rose so Doc could take her place.

"Not a problem at all, Louise. I like the night work. It gets me out of the house. Not so much time to think." He put his black bag on the bed and looked down at the sleeping boy.

Brooke reached for Mac as he went to leave. "Mac, please stay." He gave her a slight smile as she entwined her fingers with his. She draped her other arm around her mother's waist, giving it a gentle squeeze.

"He'll be okay, Mum." Brooke hoped her words were true.

Davey woke up a little grizzly when Doc removed the bedcovers.

"Davey wants Juzz Mac," he said in a sleepy voice.

Brooke released Mac so he could go and kneel by the bed.

He said, "Hey, come on, buddy. Let the Doc have a look at you and then you can go back to sleep. Okay?"

"Kay." Davey reached for Mac's hand and hung on tight. "Davey bad boy?"

"No, buddy, you're not a bad boy." Mac ran his thumb over Davey's knuckles just as he'd done with her in the café.

Doc placed a miner's lamp over his head and then proceeded to examine Davey from head to toe, checking his heart rate, temperature and blood pressure.

"Well, he doesn't seem any worse for wear after his little nightly stroll," he said rubbing Davey's hair before pulling a lollipop from his bag. "Now this is for you, Davey, to have tomorrow after breakfast. Not before, mind."

Brooke remembered getting lollipops from Doc when she was younger and smiled.

"Davey good boy." Her brother beamed.

"That you are. That you are." Doc patted his hand.

Closing his case Doc stood to take his leave. "I'll have Karen Hill call in tomorrow just to check that all is well."

Doctor Hill had arrived in Bindarra Creek a few years back and had soon become a favourite with the town's people.

Brooke gave a sigh of relief that everything had worked out and no harm had come to Davey.

She glanced at Mac, who was now sitting on the bed with Davey on his lap. Her brother had his head resting on Mac's chest, his eyes drooping, and his lollipop still clutched in his hand.

"Davey wants Mummy," he said after a moment.

Mac stood and gently lowered Davey into her mother's arms.

"Mum, you stay here with Davey. I'll see Doc Warner out. Then I'll run Mac home," Brooke said.

"Thank you, darling."

Candice followed her, Mac and Doc from the room. At the bottom of the stairs, her sister excused herself and headed in the direction of the sitting room.

"Thank you for coming, Doc," Brooke said. "Is there anything we should look for tonight with Davey?"

Doc ran a hand over his chin. "Make sure he is kept warm, we don't want to have him getting another chest infection like the last one. It takes a toll on his small body."

Davey had suffered a bad case of bronchitis earlier in the year that had left him weak for many weeks.

"Karen will be here in the morning." Doc Warner waved his goodbye and lifted himself into his four-wheel drive.

She turned to find Mac watching her.

"Um ..." Brooke indicated the stairs. "I'll just get changed then drive you home."

"I quite like what you're wearing now." He ran his eyes over her figure.

Brooke could feel heat wash over her body.

"Yes, well just the same." She gave him a nervous smile and edged closer to the stairs. "I won't be long."

***

Mac chuckled as Brooke tried to rush up the stairs in her ridiculously high-heeled shoes. But that dress. That dress would bring even a saint to his knees. *And I'm no bloody saint.*

A loud voice came from down the hall. "This was a bloody disaster. Not only couldn't you get Stafford to talk about the development, but you also showed weakness in running around looking for the kid."

Mac couldn't hear the reply, but he guessed that Fairfax was talking to Brooke's sister.

"Stop that bloody sniveling. Brooke with all her damn faults has more backbone than you."

"So what's our next plan?" a younger male voice asked.

"I'll ring Stafford in the morning and see if I can set up a meeting to salvage this bloody deal. Then take him to look over the site." Fairfax sounded exasperated.

Seconds passed before anyone spoke. Mac contemplated whether he should move a little closer, so he didn't miss anything when Fairfax spoke.

"You and Mrs Stafford seemed to be getting along quite well. Maybe she could persuade Stafford it's a good deal," replied the younger man.

Not bloody likely. Maureen had no say in Stafford and Sons, and Mac wanted it to stay that way.

"Maureen and I had a thing years ago, before I met your mother. But you're right, I have her mobile, I'll call her in the morning after I phone Stafford."

Brooke drew Mac's attention away from the conversation. She bounded down the stairs in a pair of cut-off jeans that displayed her pale toned legs and a short loose top with long sleeves that showed a hint of a firm stomach. Her hair was once again a mass of curls falling over her shoulders. The dress had been bad enough, but sitting next to her in the confines of her car while she wore this would be torture.

***

Brooke's step faltered on the stairs as she as she took in Mac's heated stare. And boy did that intent look heat up her body. *Yep, trouble with a capital T.*

"Ready?" she asked.

"As I'll ever be," he replied in a husky moan. "You going to be warm enough in that getup?"

"Sure." She put a little more emphasis on swaying her hips as they left the house.

"You're asking for trouble, princess," Mac said as he opened the passenger door and glared at her over the roof of the car.

Giggling, she slipped into the car. She sat for a moment tapping her fingers on the steering wheel before putting it into gear and taking off.

"Did you check on Davey before coming down?" Mac asked.

Good, stick to neutral topics.

"Yes, Mum had changed and was lying on the bed with him. I doubt she'll leave his side tonight."

She chewed on her bottom lip. Davey's disappearance had been a strain on her mother, physically and mentally. Her mother was going to beat herself up because she hadn't gone up to check on Davey earlier. Brooke knew this because she felt the same.

When they reached the garage, he asked, "Would you like to come in for a coffee before you head back home?"

"That would be nice," she agreed.

Driving around the back of the garage, Brooke turned off the engine. Mac's bike was parked by the stairs that led up to a landing lit by a light above the door.

"Looks like Fred got your bike back in one piece."

"Yes, thank God." He laughed.

Brooke had a feeling that letting anyone else ride his bike was a big deal for Mac. Trusting Fred with his machine so he could come home with Davey was another tick in his favour.

She slid from behind the wheel and followed Mac

up the single flight of stairs, which gave her another view of his tight butt. She sucked in a lungful of air, holding onto the stair rail to steady herself.

Mac opened the door, turned on the light and led her into a spacious open-plan kitchen, dining and sitting room. For a guy, he kept his flat very tidy. After living with Wilson, Brooke knew how messy some men could be.

"Take a seat and I'll put the kettle on." He indicated for her to take a seat on the lounge. "I'll get some banana cake. I can attest to it that it's very nice." He grinned sheepishly.

The yellow lounge that would have been popular in the seventies was a little worse for wear, but surprisingly quite comfortable.

Ugly brown and orange wallpaper covered the walls, and with a psychedelic artwork of pink, yellow, blue and orange swirls. It was enough to hurt a person's eyes. She twisted on the seat and sat on one foot as she glanced over to watch Mac move about the kitchen.

Mac turned and caught her watching. "How do you take your coffee?" he asked with a strange note in his voice, his eyes burning into hers.

She blinked to break the sexual tension that zinged between them and licked her suddenly dry lips. "Just milk, thanks."

He carried over two orange mugs and a yellow plate of banana cake. Brooke tried but failed to suppress her giggle.

"Do you find my dinnerware something to laugh at?"

"I'm sorry, but this whole scene belongs in the seventies."

"Hey, I was born in the seventies." He tried and failed to look affronted, joining her in a good laugh. "You should have seen it *before* I tidied it up."

A fit of giggles shook her body again. "You can't be serious."

"Honest to God, it was a lot worse." Handing her a steaming mug, he moved the cake to sit between them on the lounge.

"Tell me about your family," he suggested. He sat, with a leg tucked beneath him.

Surprised, she asked, "Why would want to know about them?"

He shrugged. "No reason. Family history interests me. I take it from a few things Fred said that your family has been around for a while."

"Yes, my great, great grandfather, Elijah Ingalls, was one of the first to settle in Bindarra Creek with two other families—the Morgans and Sullivans in 1839."

"There were no fights about who owned what?"

"Not with Elijah, but the Morgans and Sullivans had a feud about land rights. The animosity is still raging today. But to get the true side of the story, you'd have to talk to each family and reach your own conclusion."

They both took a sip of coffee and a slice of banana

cake.

"This is really good," she said around the cake. "You have to accept my apologies for talking with my mouth full. Haven't done that since Ellen slapped my hand when I was eight." She laughed.

"You have a great laugh," Mac said huskily, taking her by surprise. He looked at her mouth then shook his head. "Now back to your story."

She licked her lips. This could be a late night. "Elijah was given fifteen hundred acres to farm in 1839. It ran from the north and north-west of the river and included what is now Bindarra Creek. In 1842, Elijah gave a stretch of land that ran from the now Mt Ingalls Road up to River Road and Main Street for the construction of a small town. The town grew into a thriving township of ten thousand in its hay day."

Mac whistled through his teeth. "That's pretty impressive."

"Yes, it's a shame it's dwindled the way it has. Are you sure you want to know all this stuff?" she asked after taking another slice of cake and sipping her coffee.

"Yes, continue with your story. I like your voice. It's husky and *very* sexy."

She'd just taken another sip and had to place her hand over her face as she snorted coffee through her nose. "That wasn't what I expected you to say."

Talk about embarrassing.

Mac rose and retrieved a napkin for her from the

cupboard. "Sorry, didn't mean to choke you." He laughed, which crossed out his apology. He removed the cake plate and sat closer to her this time. "The story," he prompted.

"Story … right … where was I?"

"The town." He reached out and rubbed her foot protruding from under her bottom.

"Yes, the town," she said breathlessly. Her heart seemed to be doing a tap dance against her chest.

"Over the years, the Ingalls went from crops to cattle, at one time having the finest cattle station in the area. My grandpa sold the last of the land in the 1960s to open Ingalls Development. End of story," she said in a rush.

Lord, I have to stop him from continuing with his foot massage, no matter how great it feels.

She stood in a hurry, but the foot she'd been sitting on had gone to sleep, and she all but fell into his lap. Mac reached out and grabbed her as he stood.

He held her close, too close. He smelled of coffee, banana bread and spice, all very yummy things to eat. She peeked up at him through lowered lashes in time to see his hypnotic eyes watching her right back. Then he was lowering his face towards her. She stood frozen, waiting, not game enough to take a breath in case he changed his mind. Then soft, warm lips caressed hers. All the tension that had paralysed her moments before vanished and she melted into a hard chest.

He claimed her lips with primal obsession. All the

pent-up passion that had been zinging in the air between them since they met became a raging fire of desire. He lowered her to the lounge and followed her down. They lay in a tangle of arms and legs, his arousal pressed into her stomach, heat pooling between her legs. She wanted more, so much more. Tugging at his T-shirt, she pulled it from the confines of his jeans and smoothed her hands over the rippling planes of his abdomen and around to his back.

"I've wanted to do this from the moment I saw you in that Garden of Eden," he muttered.

She giggled. "Garden of Eden, huh?"

"Um um." He rained kisses along her jaw, down her neck then back up to the sensitive spot below her ear. She arched her back, pressing against him.

His hand snaked under her top, cupping her heavy breast in his hand, then rolled her nipple between his thumb and forefinger. He pushed her top up, exposing her to his hot gaze.

The loud, consistent ring of his mobile broke through the fog of desire, bringing her back to earth with a thud. She drew in ragged breaths as Mac kissed her forehead.

"I better get that," he said in a frustrated tone. He moved from the lounge and picked up his phone. "This better be bloody important, Fred."

Brooke sat up and rearranged her clothing. She had to get out of here before things went too far. She needed time to think.

"Um … I'll … err … just go," she said, inching towards the door.

"Hang on," Mac said into the mobile then placed his hand over the mouthpiece. "Yes, I'm sorry for letting things get out of hand." He gazed at her with underlying passion in his eyes.

Warmth washed over her from the tip of her toes to the roots of her hair. She'd never felt so humiliated in her life. "Yes…well."

She all but ran out the door and down the stairs to her car. Brooke sat resting her head on the steering wheel, dragging in a deep calming breath. *What was I doing? Or even thinking?* She wasn't one to have sex with someone she'd just met. After a few days maybe, but definitely not the first day. She drove back home, her thoughts a jumbled mess.

Running up the front steps to the house, she almost ran into her father.

"Where the hell have you been?" he clipped.

She should have known he wouldn't have gone to bed yet, he was a bloody prowling night owl. "I ran Mac home," she replied with a shrug.

"I want to talk to you."

Don't you always? "I'm not interested in what you have to say, Father."

She walked towards the stairs. Her foot was on the bottom step to the landing before her father spoke again.

"*Brooke*! You will speak to me now."

"What, Father? What have I done wrong now?"

She had to get away from him. She glanced over her shoulder. "I'm going to check on Mum and Davey then go to bed."

He waved a hand dismissing her words. His features softened into a light frown instead of his normal scowl. *He's after something.* She started up the stairs.

"I need you to talk to Stafford. He likes you for some reason. You have to convince him to invest in this project."

Her nostrils flared, the pounding in her ears almost deafening. She drew air into her lungs before turning back to her father. "No, Father, I don't have to speak to Roland. You do your own dirty work."

Her father glared at her. The scowl was back.

"What will you do, Father, cut my allowance? I don't need your money, I haven't touched it in years."

"No, but you do need your brother," he said, smugly. So sure he held all the cards. His eyes flared with triumph. "You will do this, Brooke, or you don't see David again."

Brooke felt her stomach lurch. He couldn't do this.

"Mum would never stop me from seeing Davey."

He raised a sarcastic eyebrow. "You wouldn't want to upset your mother with us having words. You know how important it is she has no stress, and after tonight ..." He left the rest unsaid.

Bastard!

"Think about it, girlie. I have the playing hand here, so do as I say."

He turned and walked to the back of the house. His back straight, he carried himself with pride. He had no reason to be proud. Everything he owned he'd gained from his association with Mum and Grandpa. *He's up to something, but what?* She'd see him in Hell before she let him ruin Ingalls Development.

CHAPTER FIVE

Doctor Hill, a slim woman of medium height and blonde hair, arrived early the next morning. She declared Davey none the worse for his adventure the night before. The little boy was full of energy, eager to eat his breakfast so he could have his lollipop. Brooke had Karen check her mother over, to be on the safe side. The stress of the previous night was evident in her mother's drawn features.

"Louise, I'd like you to rest up today. Your heart and blood pressure are good, but you look rather drained. No doubt you got very little sleep last night." Karen looked warmly at her mother. "I'd best be off, I have a couple more homes to visit this morning."

Brooke showed Karen to the door and thanked her for taking the time to call out to check up on Davey and her mother. After a light breakfast, she went looking for them both and found the pair on the garden patio. She smirked at the thought of Mac seeing it as the Garden of Eden.

Davey sat on the floor playing with his favourite talking figurines while her mother watched from the sofa, reading an adventure story to him.

"Mum?"

Her mother raised her eyes and smiled at her.

"Darling, thank you for this morning. I feel better knowing everything is good with both Davey and me."

"Roo, Davey play with Woody and Buzz."

"I can see that, little man."

"Davey go to see Juzz Mac today?"

"Maybe later." She was unsure of what she felt for Mac, but knew it would be better if she spoke to him herself before taking Davey to see him.

"Mum, have you decided what you plan to do with Zara?" Brooke hoped there would be no further scenes that might upset her mother.

"I let her go while you were having breakfast," her mother replied. "Davey's at school most of the day, and we see you on weekends, so there's no need for her. Why your father hired her, I'll never understand. Both Ellen and Julianne would have been capable of caring for him until I recovered."

"And she left quietly?"

"Yes, I don't think she was game to say anything after your talk to her last night. In fact, I think she was expecting it."

"Thank heavens for that." Brooke let out a breath of relief. "I thought I might call in to see Mrs Edwards sometime today. I'd like to see her before I leave."

"Ruth would love that, darling, she enjoys your visits." Her mother kept her gaze fixed on the book in her hands.

***

Brooke drove down the busy main street full of people doing their last-minute weekend shopping. When she pulled up outside the garage a few moments later, Russel Green came out to see her.

"Hi, Brooke."

"Hello, Russel." She smiled at him. "What on earth are you doing here?"

"I'm working for Fred on a Saturday. It gives me some pocket money for the week."

"Are you old enough to work? Last time I saw you, you were still chasing tadpoles." She laughed and slid from behind the wheel.

Brooke hated tadpoles—and frogs for that matter—and Russel had taken great delight in chasing her with one when she and Davey had run into him one day by the river.

"No, gave that up a while back. Now I chase girls," he told her with a cheeky grin.

Not that he'd have to do much chasing. He was a good-looking boy. Thick black curly hair, deep brown eyes and a smile that would melt any girl's heart.

"How's your mum?" she asked, resting back

against her car.

"She's good, expecting another baby in a couple of weeks. At least, she hasn't been too sick with this one."

"Good heavens. How many is that now?"

"This will be number seven. The house is starting to get pretty small." He kicked at a stone on the road. "Mac's going to teach me all he knows about being a mechanic. Fred said he'd think about taking me on as an apprentice, but I have to prove myself first."

Fred had a soft spot for anyone doing it tough. He'd taken Russel under his wing, and she was sure Mac would do the same.

"Is Mac around?"

"He's over at Beth's café getting some lunch. I'm just about to shut the garage for the day. Do you need fuel?"

Brooke looked over at the café, not sure she wanted to go over there looking for him. "Um…no, I'm fine," she said absently.

"He won't be long if you want to wait." Russel gazed towards the café. "Speak of the devil."

Mac strode across the road. His powerful legs ate up the ground beneath them, his broad chest tapering to narrow hips hugged by well-worn jeans.

Brooke placed her sweaty hands in her jeans pockets, swallowed hard and wondered what she was doing here.

Oh shoot, who am I trying to kid? I want to finish what we started last night.

Her dreams had been full of Mac, his hands whispering across her naked skin, him placing feather-light kisses where his hands had been. She gave herself a mental shake. *If I'm not careful, I'll explode in front of poor Russel.*

Mac smiled at her as he drew closer. Her stomach did some silly somersault thing.

Heavens, what those eyes do to me. "Hi," she said. *Very intelligent.*

"Hi, yourself." His eyes deepened to midnight blue. "To what do I owe the pleasure of your company again so soon?"

Crap, she hadn't thought she'd have to give a reason to be here. She couldn't say she needed fuel seeing she'd already told Russel she didn't.

"Um, I thought I'd drop by and let you know how Davey is this morning." She waved her hands about as if she was getting ready to take flight. "I was in town doing some shopping, that sort of thing."

Mac laughed deep in his throat. His tongue ran over his lips. Her gaze followed it like a dog looking at a juicy bone. Oh, to have her tongue back in his tantalising mouth. She'd nip his full bottom lip, teasing, drawing him in to deepen the experience.

She swayed and Mac reached out to catch her. He pulled her against his chest.

"You okay?"

"Yeah ... I'm ... err ... fine." She clung to him, not wanting to let go, but knowing Russel was watching the exchange.

"Come on, let's get you upstairs and see if we can't fix you up," he said, tucking her under his arm. "Russ, you right to lock up?"

"Yeah, no problem." Russel watched them with concern written over his face. "She okay?"

"Sure, she just had a big night, with her brother missing for awhile and all."

"Oh yeah, heard about that."

Thank heavens Mac had come up with a good excuse for her almost falling at his feet.

"Okay, princess, let's get you sorted."

Brooke had no argument with that, him sorting or fixing her up. There was no way she was going to tell him the only reason she had swooned was because of him and her wayward thoughts. No, better to let him think it was because of the night before.

***

"Would you like coffee?" Mac asked as he tossed his burger on the cupboard.

"No thanks. I had one with Mum before I left."

Mac ran a hand through his hair. *Damn. Now, what am I going to do?*

"Don't let me keep you from your lunch," she said in that husky voice of hers.

I need to stay away from Brooke Fairfax.

That morning he had risen with his body still humming with his residual need for her. When his normal ten kilometre run hadn't eased the tension, he'd run for another ten. By the time he'd come home, he'd felt like he was under control. Now here she was, back in his tiny flat and it felt like the walls were crowding in on him.

Yes, have lunch. That will keep my hands busy.

He grabbed his burger and they sat at the table. He took a large bite out of the bun.

"My father has given me an ultimatum," she said in a rush, taking Mac by surprise. "I either convince Mr Stafford to sign on for this deal or risk not seeing Davey again."

Mac swallowed before placing his burger back in the box. He ran a hand through his hair.

"What are you going to do?" His lunch was forgotten.

"I don't know." She stood up and began to pace the room, casting him the occasional glance. "I like Roland, he seems like a nice man. Father must be up to something if he's pushing me to help. I don't want to help him, but I'm not sure I could stand to lose seeing Davey. My biggest fear is if I tell Roland my suspicions, Davey won't understand why I'm not there for him anymore."

Tears filled her eyes and ran down her cheeks. She wiped them away with the tip of her finger.

No, not tears. I can't cope with tears.

"This is so silly of me."

Mac strolled over and took her into his arms. *Bad Move.*

"It can't be easy being put in this situation." He rubbed his cheek on the top of her head. "What about your mother? I can't see her not letting you see

Davey."

"Normally no, but Father could make life very uncomfortable for her. That's a stress she doesn't need at the moment."

She lifted her head and gazed into his eyes.

Damn. Nope, I'm no saint.

He lowered his mouth to her soft lips. His blood pounded through his veins. He opened his mouth, encouraging her to follow his lead. She tasted of coffee and smelled like sunshine. He nipped her bottom lip before deepening their kiss with unbridled passion. A groan came from deep within him. He pulled her closer to his body, molding her body to his length.

He raised a hand to her breast, bringing her nipple to a tight peak, rolling it between his thumb and forefinger.

He trailed kisses down her throat and lifted her onto the table then stepped between her legs. Pulling her T-shirt over her head, he ran his hands over her delectable body.

She was gorgeous, dusky pink nipples against pale skin. His body ached with need.

A knock on the door jarred them apart. Mac still hummed with arousal as he picked up her top from where he had dropped it on the floor and handed it to her. His jaw clenched as Brooke rushed from the room to the back of the flat.

Who in Hell could this be?

"Hang on, I'm coming," he said when a second

knock followed shortly after the first.

He hoped the evidence of his arousal would subside by the time he opened the door. Mac dropped his head to his chest and closed his eyes for a moment before opening the door wide. The last person he expected to see was his father.

His father walked past him into the room, casting a disparaging glance at the small quarters.

"Hell, Brit what in the good Lord's name possessed you to live in this place?"

"Dad, shh ..." Mac whispered to his father. "What are you doing here?"

"We need to talk business." His father turned around to face him. "Fairfax is up to his ears in something, and it's not all good. To tell you the truth, it's one of the reasons I'm here."

Mac shot a glance down the hall.

"So it wasn't because you were worried about me?" Mac teased his father. It was good to see his father. He'd missed talking to the old man. However, his timing could have been better.

His father laughed. "Yes well, it's a bit of both."

"Can we talk about this later?" Mac grabbed his father's arm, hoping to steer him to the door. "Brooke is in the bathroom."

"No, Brooke is right here," she said, her movements stilted as she walked into the room, confusion in her beautiful green eyes. "Why is Roland here? Why's he calling you Br...?"

Mac saw the moment the penny dropped for her.

Her face pale, anger flared in her eyes, turning them to a deep green.

"He's your father, isn't he? I should have worked it out. You are almost the image of each other. Why didn't I see it last night?" She glared at Mac. "Probably because there was so much happening, I didn't pick it up."

"Brooke, I can explain," he said, holding his hand out as he moved towards her.

She skirted out of his reach. "Don't come near me, Mac, or Brit, whatever your name is," she yelled, her fists clenched at her side. "You lied to me. You held me in your arms and lied to me."

"I didn't lie."

"Oh? What? Not telling me Roland is your father isn't lying?" She turned her furious eyes on his father who was watching the exchange with interest. She pointed at him. "It's something to do with my father, isn't it? It's some shonky business deal." Tears ran down her face.

Mac swallowed, feeling like every kind of heel under the sun. He stepped in front of her, his gut twisted tight. "Brooke, please, let me explain."

"No, you should have explained when I started to tell you about Father." She sidestepped him to get to the door. "You were just sucking me in, trying to get information out of me for your precious business deal. You're both just like my father. Lying, underhanded cheats!"

CHAPTER SIX

Mac glanced at his father with accusing eyes.

"I told you I would ring you, Dad," he said, running his hand through his hair. "Now look what's happened."

"Son, don't blame me for something you stuffed up."

"I didn't stuff anything up. There was nothing between us to stuff up." Mac glared at his father. "I care about Brooke as a friend. She's going through a rough time, but that's all." Why did that sound so hollow to his ears?

"For something that is so unimportant to you, you're mighty upset, son."

"Shut up, Dad. Where's Maureen? I can't see her cooling her feet while you're here talking to me."

"I put her on a plane this morning before coming here. She was happy to get away from what she calls the center of nowhere."

His father sank into one of the chairs. "I'm sorry if I messed things up for you and Brooke."

"Yeah, me too," Mac said, sitting down and ignoring the fact that he'd told his father earlier there was nothing between them.

"I like that girl," his father told him. "There's a special quality about her. An honest one so rare these days."

"Yes, she thinks highly of you too, Dad. Well, she did until she found out you were my father," he said with a short laugh then leaned forward, resting his forearms on his knees.

"So are you going to tell me what's going on with that young lady?"

"Her father has threatened to stop her from seeing Davey if she doesn't convince you to sign on for this project." Mac stood up, rubbing his jaw. He walked over to the sink and rested his hands on the bench. "I have to tell you, Dad, I'd feel pretty crap if it was my fault she couldn't see her brother anymore."

He turned and rested his hip on the cupboard, his arms crossed over his chest.

"Then we'll have to make sure that doesn't happen."

"Dad, she thinks her father is up to something."

His father nodded. "She's not the only one. Make some coffee, son, and let's get down to it."

Mac busied himself with the coffee for his father, wondering if Brooke would ever trust him again and if his feelings ran deeper than just a roll in the hay. He set the mug on the kitchen table with the remains of the banana cake.

His father reached for his mug. "I've had Steve do some background checking on Gordon Fairfax. It seems that Fairfax isn't the man's real name."

Mac lifted an ankle onto his knee and waited until his father elaborated.

"His real name is Lain Cross. In his early twenties, he was investigated for a property fraud that involved his father. The old man took the fall for the operation. Shortly after that, Lain changed his name by deed poll and moved to Tamworth. He held a position with a real estate agency before moving on to Ingalls Development. The rest you know."

Mac raised his eyebrows. "What about this deal with us?"

"He seems to have kept his nose pretty clean since he married Louise, but that could be because of her father. I think it would be best if we tread warily with Fairfax. I won't be giving him any control or access to finances."

"Just how do you plan on doing that?"

"Quite simple, I'll tell him the truth. That I never trust anyone other than myself or my son with my money."

"So you don't plan on telling him who I am?"

"Not at this stage." His father leaned back in his

chair taking a drink of his coffee. "I think it would be in our best interest if he doesn't know that information just yet. You can keep your ears open and see what his reaction is."

His father was good with the financial end of their business. It was why Stafford and Sons had done so well over the years.

"And if Brooke discloses who I am to her father?"

"We'll cross that bridge if it happens."

"Has Fairfax told you where he intends to build this thing?"

"No, not yet. I put him off on discussing it until the report came in." His father took a sip of his coffee. "The initial contract was a proposal for a housing development, and later to build a shopping complex."

"Let me know as soon as you do." Mac frowned. "I'm not comfortable with the shopping centre idea, there are too many livelihoods at stake. But the houses will bring some much-needed work into the community."

His father left with the promise to call before he came to visit in future.

Mac collected the mugs and placed them on the sink. He'd promised himself he'd never let a woman get under his skin. He'd seen friends fall to their knees over their partners only to be destroyed when the relationship ended. He'd had his affairs, but never once lost his head or heart to any of the women he'd taken to his bed.

Brooke was different—she was a forever girl. And

God help him, he still wasn't sure he was a forever guy.

***

After driving for much of the afternoon out by the vineyards, Brooke returned to Bindarra Creek and parked by the river. She had been a fool to believe that Mac would be any different to all the other men she'd had in her life. She had a long list of men who had let her down—her father, her brother, her art professor. Wilson, who had wanted her for money, not love, so he could take the fast road in her family's business. Yes, they had all let her down over the years. Maybe she should swap sides. Her friend Tyrelle was always telling her a woman's love was special, more caring.

Brooke laid her head back against the headrest of the seat and closed her eyes.

What should I do now?

She didn't want to go back to the house. There was no way she wanted to face her father again yet. Nor did she feel like driving back to Tamworth. That would mean driving past Fred's and that lying snake in the grass. Plus, once her friends knew she was home, they'd be over for a catch-up, and she didn't feel like talking.

She could go into Armidale and rent a room for the night, and then decide what she would do about her father's threat.

Turning the ignition key, she slowly pulled out of the parking area by the river. It was a shame night had fallen so quickly, normally she loved sitting by a river. It inspired her creative juices.

She had just driven out of the town limits when her mobile phone rang. She saw it was her mother, so pushed the hands-free button on her dash.

"Hi, Mum."

"Darling, where are you?" Her mother sounded a little breathless.

"I've just left town, Mum. I'm on my way to Armidale for the night. I was going to ring you when I found a motel."

"Oh darling, what for?"

"Something happened at Mac's and I need some thinking time, Mum. Do you need me to come home?"

"No, darling, it can wait until tomorrow."

"Okay, well tell Davey I'll see him tomorrow. I'll talk to you then too. Bye, Mum, love you."

Two days of stress were catching up with her. She wiped the offending dampness from her cheeks with shaking fingertips. Davey would be devastated if he couldn't see Mac again. There was always a loser when things didn't turn out right. It was so unfair that the loser would be her brother.

Damn you, Mac! Damn you to hell and back.

Brooke pulled into the car park of a motel ten minutes out of Armidale. It was in a quiet area surrounded by native trees. The building was grey stone brick that suited the location and gave a homely welcome rather than the usual clinical exterior of many of the modern motels.

Her stomach growled, reminding her she hadn't eaten since breakfast. She hoped she'd be able to get room service.

The interior was as inviting as the exterior. Furnished with charming country furniture in blue and grey, it held a pleasant calming effect. She booked in and after discovering there was no room service at that time, walked over to the restaurant to the right of the reception area.

She stood near the entrance to the restaurant and took in the spacious room. The décor had a country feel, with round timber tables covered with dark green gingham tablecloths. The table setting ranged from two to eight with matching timber captain chairs. Floral centrepieces on each table added to the charm of the room.

A neatly dressed woman in her late forties and neatly dress walked over. "Good evening, I'm Margaret, can I help you?"

"A table for one if you have any." The room seemed crowded so Brooke wasn't sure if she would be seated straight away.

"I have one at the back if that's okay. It overlooks the pool area."

"That'll be perfect."

They weaved their way through the tables to the back of the room. Brooke was just thinking how nice it would be out of the main activity when she heard her name called. Sitting at the table next to the only vacant one was Roland.

He stood as they approached him.

"Brooke, dear, it is lovely to see you again."

"Hello, Roland."

Lord, no. I don't need this.

"Oh, you two know one another?" Margaret said. "Maybe you'd like to share a table. It's no use eating alone if you can have company."

"A wonderful idea, Margaret," Roland replied.

"I wouldn't want to intrude on your time, Roland. Is Mrs Stafford not with you?"

"She left this morning. I'd love the company." He left her no choice as he pulled the spare chair out for her.

"Mr Stafford, have you placed your order yet?" Margaret asked.

"No, I wanted to have a drink first. However, you can have Charlie bring the menus over now if you like. Brooke, would you like a drink?"

"A Chardonnay would be lovely," she told Margaret.

The woman smiled and disappeared to place their orders.

"So what brings you into Armidale, Brooke?"

"I needed to get away." She fought to relax her body and ease her racing heart. "Last night when we spoke, I thought you were different to my father. But after this morning, I'm not so sure what to think. I hate being deceived. I've had that most of my life with Father."

Roland wrapped his large, warm hand around

hers. She lowered her eyes to the table not wanting him to see the hurt she felt.

"Brooke, I want to apologise," he said softly. "I know we should have told you we were related, but Mac wanted to keep it quiet."

"Why? So he could find out information about my family?" She raised her chin and glared at him.

"No, he is dealing with a lot of emotions at the moment," Roland said, removing his hand now that she was looking at him. "His brother, my youngest son, died three months ago, and Brit blames himself."

A heavy feeling sank into her chest. She fought back tears, remembering the pain she'd felt after her grandpa's death. To feel responsible for a sibling's death would be a living nightmare. Then she remembered what her father had said last night about Roland losing a son.

It was clear from the sadness in Roland's eyes that he was hurting from the loss of his younger son, but there was pain there for Mac as well. Roland thought the world of his son and wasn't afraid to show it. That was something her father would never do, show he cared for one of his children.

"I'm sorry for your loss. It can't be easy losing a child."

Charlie chose that time to arrive with the menus and Brooke's wine, telling them she would return shortly. Brooke took the time to get her thoughts together. After selecting their meals they sat in silence for a moment or two, almost as if Roland understood Brooke needed time.

"Mac told me about your father's ultimatum," Roland said.

"I'm sure he did," she said sarcastically, running her fingers up the stem of her glass. Tears gathered in her eyes again. Why should that worry her? So he'd told his father, she'd suspected he would.

"Brooke, he only told me because I raised the subject of your father first."

She snorted in an unladylike fashion and folded her arms over her chest. *Now I'm acting like a spoiled two-year-old.*

"Let me reassure you, dear. I'm quite prepared to do business with your father."

Brooke sat up straighter in her chair. *Is this man mad? Unless he is as shady as my father.*

"Roland, did Mac tell you what I think about my father?"

"Yes, but I already knew that. I've checked your father's credentials," he said with a satisfied smile. "I know all about his business dealings to back before he met your mother."

Her father never spoke of his life before Bindarra Creek. She shouldn't have been surprised that Roland had her father investigated. He was a businessman. No doubt her father had done a similar thing. "Then why are you going to do business with him?"

"Because I think the project has merit," he said, leaning back in his chair.

Brooke gazed at Roland. *Could he be speaking the*

truth? Could he be the honourable businessman I thought he was last night? A man like Grandpa? He was a quiet man, one who gave the impression of being a pushover, but it was all a cover.

"Now, what I'm going to do is tell your father we had a lovely dinner together, and that we discussed the project, thus stopping him from carrying out his threat to you, my dear."

"Roland—" Brooke went to interrupt.

"No, Davey needs you, my dear, and so does your mother. I won't be telling a lie. We are having dinner together, and we are talking about the project."

"Seems you and your son are both good at half-truths." She was grateful that he would do this for her, but all it did was bring home the fact that Mac had lied by omission. Their meal arrived and Roland changed the topic of conversation.

It wasn't until she went to her room that she realised Roland hadn't explained the reason Mac felt responsible for his brother's death. More to the point, why was Mac in Bindarra Creek? Was he investigating the business deal or was he there to deal with his grief privately?

The room was comfortable with a queen-sized bed covered in a green floral bedspread, and two upholstered chairs in one corner with a low table between them. She made herself a cup of coffee and went out onto the balcony that overlooked the garden filled with Australian native plants. The temperature had dropped, but Brooke didn't mind the nip in the air.

Sitting in one of the white wicker chairs, she thought back over the past couple days. *Thank God, we never got as far as having sex, that's all it would have been.*

She was sure if it had gone that far, she would have lost her heart completely. She'd believed she and Mac had a connection, but like most of the men in her life, he only wanted to use her.

Wilson with his wavy blond hair and dark brown eyes had told her he loved her. That she was the most precious gift he'd received, and thanked his lucky stars they'd met. When he proposed, she'd believed her life was complete.

Brooke blinked back tears. She would not feel sorry for herself. She'd done that before, and it almost destroyed her. No, she would concentrate on her art. In heartache, she found that she did her best work.

CHAPTER SEVEN

Mac walked slowly over to Beth's for a meal. He'd left it as late as possible so most of the other diners would be gone. He knew Fred would be there. Fred was always there these days. If the pair of them thought no one was taking any notice of the time they were spending together, they were wrong. Half the time people went to Beth's these days was to watch the pair together. Mac laughed and shook his head.

He entered the diner to find only a couple of stragglers left having coffee. Mac almost laughed out loud when he saw the death-glare Fred sent the group. Of course, they were a group of Fred's old friends, and Mac was sure they were lingering just to get a reaction.

"Hi, Fred." He slapped his friend lightly on the back. "What do you know?"

"Bloody nothing," Fred replied, throwing sideward glances at the group of men.

Beth walked through from the back, stopping mid-stride. "I thought you said you wouldn't be over tonight?"

"Yeah, well that didn't pan out the way I'd hoped."

"You and Brooke have a fight? Russel said she'd called in to see you," Beth persisted. If there was one thing about Beth, she was not backward in coming forward with her questions.

"Yeah, something like that." His heart raced as he remembered the expression in Brooke's eyes. It wasn't just hurt, it was devastation, and he'd put it there.

"You want to tell Granny Beth all about it?" The look of hope in her eyes had Mac chuckling.

"No, but thanks for the offer, Granny Beth. This problem is something I need to work out for myself."

The group of men at the table decided they'd had enough. They got up to leave. Fred lost interest them, too busy listening to Beth and Mac's conversation.

"Well, we're off, Beth. Thanks for the coffee and entertainment."

"Sure, boys." Beth lowered her head while Fred did a bit of huffing and puffing.

"Entertainment indeed," Fred mumbled as the door closed behind the last one. "I'll lock up before anyone else decides to come in."

Mac laughed. He'd never seen Fred move so fast.

"You want to eat with us then, Mac?" Beth asked.

"No, I don't want to intrude on the two of you. I'll just take away one of your salads."

"Intrude? What's there to intrude on? We're only having dinner," Fred said.

"I thought you might want to be alone."

Fred scratched his head. "Why would you think a dumb thing like that?"

"Jeez, I don't know, Fred. Maybe from the death-glares you were throwing your friends, the rush to shut the café."

"Oh for lamb's sake, I was glaring at them because they had done nothing but bust their chops all night. And shutting up shop for the night was because Beth hasn't had time to sit all evening."

"Well, why didn't you help her out?" Mac asked.

"Have you ever tasted my cookin', boy?" Fred asked. "She wants people to come back not take off for the hills."

Mac chuckled.

"I was fine, Mac. I had young Rosie and Ellie Fraser to help me out. They're good girls, and they work hard," she said, patting his hand. "Now come out back and I'll get us a meal. You can tell us all about you and Brooke."

The men followed Beth through to the kitchen. A table was set for two, but Beth soon moved things around to accommodate Mac. He felt a bit like a third wheel, but he wanted to talk to the pair about the Fairfax project, so now was as good a time as any.

"Take a seat, boys. Dinner won't be long."

Whatever it was, it smelled great. Beth was a damn good cook, and she often cooked a decent meal for Mac. Told him he needed to keep his strength up for work, she'd say with a wink.

"So what happened between you and the Fairfax

girl?" Fred asked.

"Brooke, her name is Brooke," Beth told him.

"Fine, what happened between you and Brooke?"

"My father." He couldn't admit to Beth and Fred what an arse he'd been. Now he'd had time to think over, he realised he should have opened up to her, especially when she'd shared her fears with him.

Fred raised his eyebrows and Beth looked at him blankly.

"Your father was in town?" Fred asked.

"Yeah, today and last night. He was the one who brought Brooke into town to look for Davey."

Beth placed a plate of hot stew and a bowl of garlic bread on the table.

"Okay, I'm lost here. The gentleman who was with Brooke last night is your father. I thought he was a friend of the Fairfax family," Beth said.

"No, Fairfax wants him to go into business on a project with him." Mac picked up his fork and dug into the tempting meal.

The conversation over the meal turned to idle chitchat, from the weather to Fred's gout, and most of the time the couple had Mac laughing at their antics.

"Well, that was another great meal, Beth, thank you." Mac rose to put his plate in the dishwasher. Beth waved her hand for him to sit back down.

"You sit there, boy. I can do that."

Mac sighed, but refused to do as she asked. "Beth, you've been on your feet all day, served up a wonderful meal, the least I can do is clear the dishes."

He gathered Fred and Beth's plates as he went, rinsed all three and loaded the dishwasher. Filling three mugs with fresh coffee, he placed them on the table before taking his seat again.

"So your father is a high-flyer like Fairfax, and you're just a mechanic?" Beth asked.

"Not quite, but I can talk to you about that another time. One of the reasons I came over tonight was I wanted to discuss the Fairfax project." Beth and Fred exchanged a glance. "I take it by those looks you've heard a bit about it."

"A little. Roy Towns—he's one of the councillors— mentioned something the other day, but said it was all hush hush," Beth told him.

Mac nodded. "Nothing is settled between Dad and Fairfax yet, but Dad is looking into it all a bit further."

"So what's all this got to do with us?" Fred asked.

"What has this councillor told you?" Mac asked Beth. It would be better to find out exactly how much they knew before going into all the details.

"Not a lot, merely that Fairfax had big plans for the town, and to be prepared for a lot of changes." Beth shrugged. "To tell the truth, I was run off my feet at the time, so I didn't take a whole lot of notice. It wasn't until I mentioned it to Fred that we wondered what was going on. Roy hasn't been back in again, so I haven't been able to push him more for information."

"What Fairfax is proposing is to develop a new subdivision, and he wants to build one of those shopping complexes here in town," Mac said.

Fred and Beth stared at each other then back at Mac, their brows furrowed.

Mac stood and moved to the sink, leaning his back against it. Fred reached for Beth's hand and gave it a light squeeze.

"I've told Dad I'm not happy about the shopping centre idea. If Fairfax pushes for the centre to go ahead, we can start a petition and submit it to the council. We'll have the whole town behind us on this one." Mac knew a development like this could well mean the death of small businesses like Fred and Beth's. They'd never be able to afford the inflated rent Fairfax would be bound to ask for.

"I should have known you'd do something like this, Mac," Fred said as he stood and ambled over to where Mac stood. He extended his hand.

Mac accepted the handshake, but was surprised when Fred pulled him forward into a bear hug. It was the first time he'd ever seen Fred show any emotion.

"So when will you know all the details?" Beth asked with a smile back on her face.

"Dad is going to call Fairfax for a meeting tomorrow. We're not sure Fairfax will go along with our terms."

"Does this mean you'll be leaving us, son?" Fred removed his cap to scratch his head.

Mac shook his head. "No, Dad wants me to hang around here and keep an eye on things. I need to ask you both not to reveal who I am at this stage. I'll keep working at the garage, Fred, if that's okay? And remain as Mac, the mechanic." Moreover, that would give him time to make things right between him and Brooke.

"Fine by me, son. You've taken a load off me working in the garage, and it's left me with more time to concentrate on other important things." He threw Beth a cheeky wink that made her blush.

It was all quite sweet, Mac thought. As long as he didn't think about what they had planned for the rest of the night.

"Well, we'll keep our ears to the ground and fill you in on anything we find out. Right, Fred?" Beth said as she stood to put the remains of the dinner in the fridge.

"Uh, err yeah sure, sure," Fred, replied absently.

Mac noted Fred watching Beth with a gleam in his eye.

"I'll get out of your hair now. Enjoy the rest of your evening." Mac made a run for the door.

***

Brooke had a quick breakfast the next morning before she returned to the family home. She hoped her mother would let Davey come with her to Tamworth for the week. With school holidays started, there were a lot of activities taking place that Davey would enjoy. She felt guilty for not returning home the night before and hoped this would make it up to her brother. The only obstacle would be her father.

She hadn't seen Roland that morning as she'd checked out, so she had no idea if he'd spoken to her father or not. What if Roland changed his mind? There was no way her father would let her take Davey, for no other reasons than to spite her.

After pushing the keypad, she drove through the gates and pulled up in front of the house behind Roland's car. Her father and Roland were standing on the veranda shaking hands, so she gathered they must have agreed to the terms of the business.

"Good morning, my dear," her father greeted her.

Butterflies assaulted her stomach. That had to be a good sign, he never called her 'my dear', hell he never called anyone 'my dear'.

"Father, Roland, it is lovely to see you again." She could play this game. She'd seen her father and siblings do it many times. Smile politely, make small talk and suck them in—her father's motto.

"Brooke, it's always a delight to see you. Thank you for the pleasure of your company last night. It was a delight to dine with you."

"Thank you, Roland. If you'll both excuse me, I'd like to speak to Mum before I leave for Tamworth."

She hurried up the front steps, her nerves wound tighter than a spring. *God, I hate this place when Father is home.* It was like Doomsday had fallen over the house.

"Brooke," her father called.

Brooke pivoted on her heels, a syrupy smile plastered on her lips. "Has Roland left?"

"Yes, I want to thank you for talking Stafford around. This development is important to ... err ... the business."

Brooke lowered her head, not wanting her father to read her expression.

"Once the subdivision is complete, we can start on the shopping complex."

She jerked her head up. "What shopping complex?"

"I'm going to build one of those big shopping centres on the outskirts of town."

"Over my dead body!" She narrowed her eyes. "You will kill the town. Main Street will become deserted. Think of the people who will suffer."

Irritation flared in her father's eyes. "They can bloody rent space in the centre."

"What with?" She spread her hands. "I won't allow you to do it, Father. People are trying to rebuild the town, not destroy it."

He grabbed her arm in a tight vice-like grip. "You have nothing to do with this, girlie. Keep your nose out of my business."

"I will stop you, mark my words." She reefed free from her father's hold and went in search of her mother.

Her father's incessant swearing followed her through the house. She only hoped she hadn't caused more problems for her mother. The front door slammed shut as he left. Her mother and Davey came out from the kitchen as she walked through the sitting room.

"Roo!" Davey cried with excitement as he ran

towards her, dressed in jeans and a *Buzz Lightyear* T-shirt. It seemed *Toy Story* was his favourite this week.

"Hello, little man. Hello, Mum." Lifting her brother for a quick hug, she popped him on the floor again.

Her mother took a seat on the sofa by the window that overlooked the back garden. "Brooke, darling, I'm glad you're home. We need to have a talk."

She leaned down and kissed her mother's cheek.

"Yes we do, Mum. Davey, can you go and ask Ellen if she would mind making me a cup of coffee?"

That was the housekeeper's cue to keep Davey occupied for a while. It worked every time. She'd get Davey to help her set a tray, ready for Brooke and her mother, so they'd have time to talk in private.

"Kay," he said as he raced towards the kitchen arms spread wide. "To infinity and beyond!"

"Sit here, dear." Her mother patted the seat next to her.

Brooke did as her mother asked.

"Your father told me last night that he planned to stop you from seeing Davey unless you agreed to his terms."

"Yes." Brooke swallowed the lump in her throat. "But as you probably know, Roland has decided to do business with Father. Mum, do you know anything about Father building a shopping complex in town?"

"No, he hasn't said anything to me about it. Oh, Brooke, that would cripple the Main Street traders."

"I've told him I won't allow it. I'm going to ring

Clarence Lansky to see if he's aware of the proposal."

"Yes, I think that would be the best way to go." Her mother clasped her hands in her lap. "Brooke, your father and I are separating. I told him last night he will need to find somewhere else to live."

Brooke stared at her mother in disbelief. At last, her mother would be free. *I should have been here. Instead, I was selfishly worrying about my wounded pride, and Mum was dealing with this.*

"That can't have gone down well." Brooke reached for her mother's hand.

"Let's just say your father plans to fight for all he can get, as well as the house and part of the business." Her mother gazed out over the garden. "When he finds out that the business is tied up in a trust and you're the trustee, he won't be happy. Nor will Candice and Duncan."

"But you have a prenup. So the business and house are no concern to him legally." Brooke reminded her mother.

"He's going to fight that as well."

"Lord, this is not going to end well," Brooke said slowly.

When her Grandpa learned he had cancer, he'd set up a trust fund for the business with Brooke as the trustee. In his will, each of his grandchildren received a sum of money and shares in the business. Davey's share was in a trust fund in her mother's control. Grandpa had never liked her father and had refused to leave him anything. Her mother had received shares in the business and a sizable sum of money. Brooke received the family property.

"What do you want to do, Mum?"

"I want you to take Davey to Tamworth with you. I'm going to speak to your father, Candice and Duncan tomorrow, and tell them the full extent of the will."

Brooke swallowed, her throat dry. "Maybe I should stay, Mum. I don't like the idea of you facing the three of them alone."

"I have Mathew and Ellen here. Your father wouldn't dare do anything while they're around. Candice might be hurt, but she's a good girl at heart. She's always tried to please your father."

Just like I used to when I was a child. "And Duncan?"

"I can handle Duncan."

Davey came running into the room in front of Ellen. "Len has tea and cookies," he announced, clapping his hands together and crawling up onto the sofa between the two women.

"So is Miss Brooke right to take the little one?" Ellen asked.

Brooke wasn't surprised that her mother had spoken to Ellen about her plan. The women had been friends for years as well as employer and employee. The only reason Ellen and Mathew stayed working there was because of her mother.

"I was going to ask if I could take Davey for a few days anyway." Brooke smiled. "Sit down and have some tea with us. You can tell me how Ava is doing."

They chatted for an hour about Ellen's daughter and her new grandson.

CHAPTER EIGHT

Mac didn't normally work on Sundays, but the part for Mrs Edwards' car had arrived, and he needed something to keep his mind off Brooke. The revving of an engine caught his attention. Walking to the front of the garage, he found black smoke billowing from the exhaust of a black sedan.

"Can I help you?" he asked as a tall, dark-haired man unfolded himself from the car.

"Yeah, I'm not sure what's wrong with it. The engine started blowing smoke when I hit town. I was hoping you could take a look at it for me."

"Sure, pop the bonnet."

Gordon Fairfax pulled in behind the car. *Great, now what's bloody wrong?*

To Mac's surprise, he addressed the person from

the sedan.

"I've been ringing you all morning. What's wrong with your bloody phone?"

"Nothing, I've had it turned off. I do have a life away from you, you know, Dad."

That answered a couple of questions. So this was Duncan Fairfax. He was nothing like Brooke or her sister. It was obvious he took after his father's side of the family.

"What's wrong with the car? It's bloody new."

"How do I know? That's why I brought it here."

Mac leaned against the doorframe, watching the exchange. You never knew what you'd find out just by listening. It was easy to see the resemblance between the men now that he knew they were related. They both carried that same arrogance as if the world owed them.

"Well get in the Bentley and we'll go to the office. We have some problems with the Stafford deal. Your mother wants a divorce."

"When did Mother drop that little bombshell?"

"Last night," Gordon grumbled.

"Well I can't make it right now. I have another engagement. Tell me what the problem is and I'll work something out."

Fairfax glared at his son. Duncan was either stupid or knew how to handle his father. Mac had a feeling it was the former.

Their conversation plucked Mac's curiosity. So his father had been out to see Fairfax already.

He straightened and said, "If you'll excuse me, I'll take the car in and have a look at it while you two discuss your business." Mac could listen better unobserved from inside the garage.

Mac drove the car into the garage, stepped out to linger at the opening of the door and pretended to look for tools.

"So what's the problem? Stafford's on board, isn't he?"

"Yeah, yeah, Brooke finally did something right in her life. Seems she had dinner with the old guy last night and got him to agree," Fairfax gloated. "If you ask me, I think the old fart wants a piece of her arse."

They laughed. Mac ground his teeth. Any thought that his father would chase after a woman young enough to be his daughter was ridiculous, and it was more than a little degrading towards Brooke. Mac frowned. His father had dinner with Brooke last night. Why hadn't he said anything this morning when he rang?

"So I ask again. What's the problem?" Duncan said with an air of impatience.

Yep, definitely stupid. Mac expected Fairfax to hit his son about his ears any second.

"It seems Stafford will only go ahead if there are two signatures on the project account. One must be mine and the other either his or the son's. It's the way he runs his business arrangements, and both signatures have to be on any withdrawals."

"That could be a problem for us."

"Exactly, I didn't even know anything about another son. It was your job to find out. What do you know about him? I thought you said he was dead."

"The younger one is. The older is a bit of a high-flyer, well respected. He had a thing going with some top model until a few months ago. Seems he's taken off to parts unknown since the breakup."

Mac snorted. *Yeah, like I'd run off because of some woman. No woman has that kind of control over me.* He glared at the wrench in his clenched hand. *What about Brooke?*

"Good, good, so we only have the old fellow to worry about."

Mac's gut twisted as they continued their conversation. It seemed the apple didn't fall far from the tree.

"So how do we get control of the account?"

"We'll do some research on Stafford and his son. See if we can't find something to hold over their heads. Everyone has skeletons in their closets, let's find theirs."

The only secret he and his father had was Garry's drug problem. Not that that could hurt the company, but it could hurt his father if it became common knowledge.

The low hum of a smaller car caught Mac's attention.

"Makes sense to me," Duncan replied. "Okay, my lift's here. I'll catch up with you later."

Mac crossed to the SAAB and lifted the bonnet. He

had his head under it looking at nothing in particular when Duncan entered the workshop.

"How long do you think you'll need her?"

"Not sure yet. Leave me your number and I'll call you in an hour or so," Mac said.

"Make it a couple of hours, eh." He laughed and handed Mac his business card before leaving. By the look of the woman leaning against the small hatchback, he had a good idea how the Fairfax heir intended to spend his time.

Mac stalked out of the garage and watched Brooke's brother leave. He rang Steve Zenox and asked him to make sure any paper trail that could lead to Garry's drug problem was tidied up. That just left Maureen. Whether she'd open up to Fairfax already was anyone's guess.

He ended the call and looked up as a familiar blue Porsche turned onto Main Street. Adrenaline rushed through him like a torrid river. *Brooke.*

***

Davey had chatted away eagerly about what they could do during he stayed with her as Brooke drove through town on their way to Tamworth. As they neared the garage, Davey started to perform, wanting to stop and see Mac.

"Not today, sweetheart, maybe another day." Brooke hoped against hope that Davey would accept her decision, but any hope ran out the window when Davey saw Mac standing in front of the workshop.

"Juzz Mac, Davey see Juzz Mac."

"Davey we ne—" Too late. Mac had seen her car and was waving at them. "Crap."

She pulled over to where Mac was standing. *Overgrown oaf probably thinks I was coming to look for him.* She lowered her window half way.

"Juzz Mac!" Davey yelled, full of excitement at seeing his new friend. "Davey going to Roo's."

Mac leaned against the car roof and glanced inside. "Hello, Davey, Brooke." He gazed at her with regret in his eyes and Brooke's heart almost melted, but she forced herself to remember that he had deceived her. *The lying rattlesnake.*

"Mac," she said, controlling her voice so as not to upset Davey.

"About yesterday."

If looks could kill, you'd be dead by now, you lily-livered baboon.

"Juzz Mac," Davey insisted.

Mac laughed, but Brooke remained stony-faced. She was over that little game. *Yeah, whatever.* "Davey, we need to go. I have some shopping to do on the way home."

Mac glanced at her again as if searching her eyes for some sign of forgiveness. To her surprise, she had to bite her tongue to stop herself from saying something stupid like 'I love you'. *Crap, where did that come from? Gotta stop saying crap.*

Why did he have to be a liar? Davey hero-worshipped him. He'd been so caring on Friday night. They say kids knew when someone was good, right?

Lord, she was so confused.

"Well, we'll see you some other time, Mac." She wound her window up so fast she almost took his fingers off, but she needed to get out of there—quickly.

This is stupid, there's no way I'm in love with Mac. Hell, she'd only known him a few days. You don't fall in love with people in just a few days. It takes time. You need to get to know them, understand them, get used to their annoying habits.

As she sped off, she looked in the rear-view mirror to see Mac run his hand through his hair. *No, there's no way I'm in love with him.* Even if she were, well, she'd just have to un-love him. That's all there was to it.

Forcing a smile on her face for Davey, she started to sing along with the CD, knowing it wouldn't take long for Davey to join in. He loved singing and knew that whenever he was with her, he could sing at the top of his voice and not get into trouble for being noisy. So they sang off-key to the sounds of Katy Perry.

Two hours later, they pulled into Brooke's driveway. The two-storey log cabin was positioned in the centre of the acre block. A garden curved around to the front of the house. She loved living here, it was far enough out of Tamworth to have some privacy, but close enough to the shops.

Her friend Tyrelle Lancaster sat on the veranda in one of her egg chairs suspended from the roof.

Tyrelle had her short brown hair spiked with purple highlights. Being short and slim—almost childlike—gave her friend a fairy-like aura. She came down the stairs with a wide smile. Green cargo pants sat on her hips, and she wore a cropped T-shirt emblazoned *Gay and Proud of it.*

"Hiya, man," she greeted Davey.

"Hiya, dude," he replied with a big grin.

Her friend and Davey had a run down on how they greeted one another, with a secret handshake and all. They always finished with a duck waddle, bumping hips for good measure.

"To what do we owe the pleasure of your company, Master Davey?"

"Davey stay with Roo." His face lit up like a thousand-watt light bulb. If Tyrelle was going to be around during his stay, it was all the better for Davey. Her brother ran up the stairs to climb into the seat Tyrelle had vacated.

"How was your trip home?"

"The usual—fights, sexual attraction, more fights," Brooke replied with a shrug.

"You had sex?" Tyrelle raised her eyebrows.

Grinning, Brooke unloaded the groceries she'd bought on her way home and handed them to her friend, then grabbed their luggage and followed Tyrelle up the stairs.

Brooke unlocked the front door. She sighed as she glanced around the room. *It's good to be home.*

The open plan room with a spacious lounge and

dining room opened out onto a wide patio. A large L-shape cream leather lounge stood in the middle of the room. An entertainment unit was positioned against the wall between two sets of large sliding doors, and a large archway led into the timber kitchen at the back of the room behind Brooke's study.

Davey ran in and raced up to the second floor. "Davey going to toilet, Roo."

"Okay, sweetheart." She dropped the suitcases beside the stairs.

"So about the sex," Tyrelle persisted.

"No, it didn't get that far. We fooled around then had a fight," Brooke told her friend with an off-handed shrug. "Now I wish I'd never met the guy."

Tyrelle and Brooke had been friends since boarding school, and she was the one person Brooke could talk to about any of her problems. They were each other's confidantes.

"I want to know it all. How'd you meet? What's he like? Is he sexy? Don't answer that, of course, he's sexy. Who is he?"

Her friend placed the groceries on the kitchen bench then came back into the lounge.

"Do I get to answer any of these questions? Or are you just going to keep adding to the list?" Brooke laughed.

"Sorry."

Brooke walked over and opened the curtains to the tranquil setting of her garden. Tyrelle fell onto the lounge. Davey returned and scrambled up beside her, laying his head on her lap.

"So who is this guy?"

"Mac—"

"Juzz Mac," Davey murmured. "Davey like Juzz Mac."

"Do you, sweetheart?" Tyrelle ran her fingers through Davey's hair.

It wasn't long before he fell asleep. The drive had tired him out. Grabbing a pillow to place under his head, Tyrelle stood and pushed Brooke into the small kitchen.

Brooke always found comfort in her kitchen. The bright yellow walls reminded her of Spring. She put the cold items into the fridge and started to unpack the rest, until Tyrelle edged Brooke onto one of the stools and demanded all the information.

"I want details, lots of details."

Brooke had to laugh at her friend's wide eyes. They resembled saucers at the moment.

Tyrelle rested her forearms on the counter, ready to take it all in. There was one thing about Tyrelle that never failed to amaze Brooke, and that was her excitement for learning all about Brooke's sex life or lack thereof.

"There's not much to tell. I saw a guy with a great body and he was nice to Davey. I told him what a shithead my father is and what he planned to do with his prospective business partner, only to find out he was the son of said business partner. I thought we had a connection, but I guess I was wrong again."

"Ouch."

"Yes, well, I said a bit more than that."

Brooke stood, ready to make coffee, but her friend motioned for her to sit. Tyrelle proceeded to make the coffee as she gave Brooke a rundown on the state of her own love-life. She and her girlfriend had called things off. Not that Brooke was surprised. Lindy was not the most giving person. She was more of a taker. The more Tyrelle was prepared to give, the more the other woman took.

"So I take it this thing is finished?" her friend asked, coming back to the subject of Mac.

Brooke rested her chin in her cupped hands on the bench and sighed. "Yes, well and truly finished."

Tyrelle placed a coffee on the breakfast bar and sat on the stool next to her. "Tell me more."

"Tyrelle, I'm not going to go into the details of my sex life."

"What sex life? You've had none for so long."

"Yes, well, it looks like it's going to be a lot longer before I think about taking that road again." Her eyes filled with tears. *How stupid, it wasn't as if he'd said he loved me or anything.*

"He hurt you, didn't he?"

"It's not that. It's not even that he's Roland's son. If he'd told me up front who he was, I would have gladly told him about Father. He didn't give me that choice, and that is what has upset me so much." She wiped the tears from her cheeks. "I've never opened myself up to anyone like I did Mac and I doubt I will again. So I'm destined to stay on my own for the rest of my life."

Tyrelle looked at her, confused. "What the hell are you talking about?"

"There will never again be anyone who turns me on the way Mac does," Brooke said and hung her head.

"What about what's-his-face?"

Brooke lifted her head. "Wilson?" At Tyrelle's nod, she continued. "I thought he was the sexiest guy alive at the time, but he's nothing compared to Mac. And it's not all about the sexual attraction. I connected with Mac on a level I've never reached with anyone else."

She rubbed a spot near her chest bone. *Christ, it hurts so much.*

***

Mac rang Duncan Fairfax to let him know his car wouldn't be ready until the following day. He closed the garage and rang his father to bring him up to date with his knowledge of the Fairfax deal. He also informed him about Fairfax looking for skeletons to hold against them and explained about his call to Steve.

"Maureen won't say anything to Fairfax. She hasn't even told her sister, and you know how close they are," his father said.

Mac felt a lot more at ease after speaking to him. Now all he had to do was put Brooke out of his mind and get on with the business at hand. *Who the hell am I kidding?* There was no way to put her out of his mind. She lived in every corner of it—her smell, the feel of her, her soft moans when he kissed her. He could still taste her on his lips. No, Brooke Fairfax would not be that easy to remove from his head.

CHAPTER NINE

Brooke received a phone call from her sister just after lunch on Monday. It seemed that the conversation with their mother had not gone well for her father or siblings. Candice was not happy and their father was talking about legal action.

"I don't know what game you're playing at, Brooke, but let me tell you now you won't get away with it," Candice hissed down the line.

"Candice, I have no idea why you're so upset. You got what you wanted from Grandpa, so stop belly-aching."

She could hear Candice's breathing getting heavier over the phone. "I'll tell you what I'm upset about, Daddy promised to leave the house to me. As the eldest, I'm entitled to it."

Brooke rubbed her temple where a headache was developing quickly. She was tired, her sleep last night interrupted with dreams of Mac and the passion that had flared between them then the argument that had followed. Over and over, it went. She needed to get some sleep or she'd be no good for anything tomorrow, plus she wanted to work on the portrait of her mother and Davey, so she had it completed for her mother's birthday.

"Candice, it was Grandpa's decision to leave the house to who he wanted."

"Now Mum will lose everything," Candice told her scathingly. "Daddy's going to hire a good lawyer and wipe the floor with her."

What happened to the kind-hearted sister who'd helped their mother on Friday? It was almost as if she never existed. Brooke had never heard her sister speak with so much disgust toward their mother before. They didn't always get along, but she'd always thought Candice loved their mother.

"Well, Candice, all I can say is good luck to you both." She hung up and dialed her mother's mobile.

"Hello, darling."

"Mum? Are you okay?"

"Yes, dear." She had to admit her mother did sound in high spirits, as if a huge weight had been lifted off her shoulders. "Your father has moved out, so there's only Ellen, Mathew and I here. I believe he's flying down to Sydney this afternoon to see some hotshot lawyer."

"Do you want Davey and I to come home? Tyrelle has taken him out for the day and planned to have him overnight, but I can ring her to change our plans."

"No, dear, I'd like you to keep Davey away for the moment. As long as you don't mind?"

Brooke began to pace the living area, rubbing her temple as she walked. "Mum, Davey is fine here, but I don't like the idea of you being there on your own."

"Darling, I'm not on my own. Mathew and Ellen are here with me."

That didn't fill Brooke with a lot of confidence. If her father decided to play hardball, there would be nothing they could do to stop him.

"Mum, I'm going to ring Stewart Hall. He might have someone who can stay on the grounds with you."

"Brooke, there is no need for that. Your father won't do anything stupid."

"Maybe not, but it would make me feel a lot better. I'll call you back in a minute."

She hung up from her mother and rang her friend Stewart, who owned a security business in Bindarra Creek. After speaking to him, she called her mother back.

"Mum, Stewart will be out there soon, he's going to update the security system in the house as well as the perimeters. They'll change the code for the gate too, so it has to be opened from the main house."

"Brooke, there is no need—"

"Yes, Mum, there is. Stewart will have someone patrol the grounds tonight. Tomorrow we can discuss permanent arrangements. I'm not going to argue with you about this, Mum. I've also asked him to change the locks and security system on both Ingalls Development offices. That will be done this afternoon before Dad has the chance to remove any documents."

Brooke ended the call, relieved to know her mother would be in safe hands.

***

Mac was still working on Duncan Fairfax's car when the obnoxious upstart swaggered into the garage.

"How's it going?" he asked abruptly.

Mac lifted his head from under the hood. "Excellent, the exhaust should be here shortly. I'm giving her an oil change and service now."

"So it'll be right to go this afternoon?"

"Yeah ..."

The ringing of Duncan's phone interrupted them.

"Yeah? Dad, no I won't be able to get to Brooke until tonight." Duncan strode to the workshop entrance. "Dad, I'll make sure Brooke sees reason."

At the mention of Brooke's name Mac froze, barely breathing as he strained to hear.

"What are you talking about? Why would Mum hire security guards?"

That was interesting. What could be going on out at the estate that would make Louise hire security guards?

Duncan leaned against the doorframe, his back to Mac, unaware that his conversation could be overheard, or maybe he just didn't care. After all, Mac was just the hired help.

"Dad, settle down. If you'd kept your temper under control this morning instead of making threats against Mum and Brooke, things would have been fine."

Every muscle in Mac's body tensed, at the thought of Gordon Fairfax threatening Brooke. No way would he let anyone hurt her.

"Dad, I'll speak to Brooke tonight. She'll see our side of things." He paused. "I won't take no for an answer. I'll get the deeds to the house and get her to give us control of the business. Don't worry."

None of the conversation made sense to Mac, except he'd gained the strong impression Brooke could be in danger. Duncan ended the call and turned to Mac, who was wiping his hands on an oily rag and pretending to study the engine.

"I want that finished by four. There'll be an extra thousand in it if you get it ready to go sooner." With that said, Duncan left the workshop and climbed into the waiting car. The same woman from the day before was behind the wheel.

There were two ways Mac could work this, he could get the jerk's car finished and go to Brooke's himself, or he could disable the car, so Fairfax had no way of getting to Brooke. Of course, then there was the risk of Fairfax hiring someone else to scare Brooke into submission.

In the end, Mac had the car done ahead of time. He called Duncan to tell him the car was ready and advised Fred to collect the bonus payment. He decided to go out to Ingalls Estate to get directions to Brooke's house. It would put his mind at rest if he knew Louise was safe too.

When he pulled up in front of the closed gates, he whistled. Some over-muscled guy he'd never seen before was working on the locking system, but he quickly stopped and gave Mac the third degree before allowing him to enter the property. What was going on here? The place was set up like Fort Knox.

***

Brooke was reading when someone hammered on the front door. The last person she expected to find standing on her doorstep when she opened it was Mac.

She stiffened. "What do you want?"

He pushed past her not waiting for an invitation.

"Your brother is on his way to see you."

"Yes, I know. The question is how do *you* know?" Her knees almost buckled from under her. *Lord, he looks so good in his bike leathers. Too good.*

He glanced around the room before bringing his gaze back to rest on her. He must have noticed something in the way she was staring at him because his eyes dilated and he moved closer to her.

"Where's Davey?" he asked in a deep tone.

"With a friend for the night."

Mac let out a groan then pulled her into his embrace before taking her mouth passionately. One hand tangled in her hair while the other drew her closer to his hard body. Brooke knew she should be resisting, but it felt so like coming home—his smell, the feel of his muscles under her touch, all so familiar. He gathered her to him, his hand roaming over her back, pulling her closer still.

She opened to him, accepting his hot, tongue-thrusting kiss. He tasted of mint and coffee, and she couldn't get enough of him. However, through the haze of lust, reality pushed its way forward. She tore her mouth from his, breathing heavily.

"No, stop." She pushed out of his arms. "I don't want this with you. Get out of my house."

Mac glared. "I'm not going anywhere, Brooke. I'm staying right here while your brother comes to talk with you."

"Oh, Mac that is just plain ridiculous. Duncan just wants to talk."

Mac sauntered over to the sofa where her book lay. "Yeah, I know what he wants. I heard him talking to your father earlier this afternoon."

Brooke's stomach rolled, leaving a nauseating taste in her mouth. Duncan was coming because of her father. She should have known it was all to do with the upheaval from this morning. Duncan and Candice had always followed their father's lead.

Her headache was getting worse. She rubbed her

temple against the growing pain. She'd need to take something for it. Thank heavens Tyrelle had taken Davey to the marsupial park in Tamworth for the day.

"It doesn't matter why Duncan is coming over, I don't want you here. Please leave." She went into the kitchen for painkillers.

"I'm not going anywhere, Brooke. I heard him make threats against you. I'm staying put." He followed her, leaned against the breakfast bar and folded his arms over his chest. All that did was draw Brooke's attention to the power of his arms. "Do you have a headache?"

"Yes...you." She swallowed two tablets. "Duncan won't tell me what's on his mind if you're here, and I'll never know what they're up to."

Mac glanced around the room. Brooke could see his mind ticking over. By the way he'd set his jaw, there was no way she was going to get him out of here. She accepted that now. She looked at the clock and realised Duncan would be arriving soon.

"Very well, if you won't leave you can wait in the study." She pushed him towards the door of the room. "But keep quiet and let me handle things. If I need your help, I'll call you."

"Okay, but if I think you're in danger at any time I'm coming out."

Brooke pulled the door slightly closed after him. She wiped her sweaty hands on her jeans. A loud knock echoed through the room as she headed to the kitchen. She placed a hand over her stomach and drew in a deep breath to steady her nerves. *Lord, I need a drink.*

Opening the door to her brother, she forced a pleasant smile on her face. *Best not to let him realise I know why he's here.*

"Duncan," she greeted. "Come in."

He strode into the house, every bit the big man. Or so he liked to believe. He surveyed the room as Mac had only her brother's movements were jerky. A light gleam of sweat covered his face.

"Davey isn't here. He's gone out with Tyrelle."

"Good. We have something we need to sort out."

Duncan sat on the lounge. He scowled, a determined set to his jaw. *So much like Father.* Brooke realised she was in for a long battle.

"What is so important, Duncan?" Brooke took the seat across from him. She would not let him think he had control of the situation.

"It's to do with Grandpa's will."

"Ah, Mother said she planned to tell you everything."

"Brooke, don't play games with me."

Leaning back in her chair, she crossed her arms over her chest. "So what do you want to talk about?"

"You know as well as I do that as the eldest grandson, I should be entitled to the bulk of Grandpa's estate." He poked his chest with his thumb.

"No, I don't know that, Duncan. I find it interesting that you and Candice both want the lion's share of Grandpa's legacy."

She resisted the urge to squirm in her seat. It was one thing to show an outward sign of bravado, but quite another to feel it. In his present state, Duncan could do anything. It was obvious he'd had a hit before coming out to her house. His glazed eyes stared at her, almost unfocused, and he fidgeted in his seat like he couldn't stay still for a moment. *I never thought I'd say it but,* thank God, *Mac is here*.

Duncan's eyes flared with jealousy. "Candice? Why the hell does she think she's entitled to it all?"

"She's the eldest grandchild." She shrugged.

"Well, she's wrong. Everyone knows that the eldest son or grandson should inherit the larger portion."

Brooke laughed at the stupidity of that answer. "Duncan, it's not the dark ages. Grandpa had the right to leave his estate to whomever he wished."

Duncan stood and paced the floor. He turned and glared down at her. Not wanting to be at a disadvantage, she stood so she was as near to eye level with her brother as possible.

He pointed a finger at her and moved closer, so he towered over her. "This is what you're going to do, Brooke. You'll sign everything over to me and there will be no problems for you or Mother."

With her body rigid, Brooke stood toe-to-toe with him. *He's just overstepped the line.*

"No, this is what's going to happen, Duncan. You're going to leave my house now and tell Father that his threats have no effect on me. If anything happens to

Mum or Davey, the law will come down on the three of you like a ton of bricks."

"Brooke, don't cross us," he said through clenched teeth. "You'll be sorry. Only you and I know about this conversation."

"No, that's where you're wrong, Duncan. I said Davey was out. I didn't say I was on my own. Mac," she called over her shoulder.

Mac walked out of the study and stood by Brooke.

Duncan gave a harsh laugh. "What, you screwing the help now, Brooke?"

"That's my business."

"This isn't the end of things."

Duncan stormed out of the house. The slamming of the door made the windows rattle. Brooke and Mac stared at each other for a moment.

"I don't think you should be here alone with Davey." Mac frowned.

Brooke paced across the room before turning to stand by the windows that overlooked her backyard. The normally peaceful view did nothing to calm her nerves. Her stomach churned with a mixture of fear and disappointment. She'd believed Duncan had wanted to make peace. *Fool that I am.* Tears slipped down her cheeks. She wiped her face angrily.

***

Mac watched as her shoulders hunched, defeated. She was a strong woman, but it would be hard to cope with the malice her family dished out in her direction. He walked over to stand behind her, wrapping his arms around her. She tensed for a moment then relaxed back against his frame.

"You know, I thought he wanted to help." She shook her head. "How stupid can a person be?"

"I don't think it's stupid to want your family to side with you."

He kissed the top of her head. What he wanted to do was lay her on the sofa and make love to her, but now was not the time. If he wanted this relationship to go further, he needed to be her friend. For the first time in his life, Mac felt he could have what his parents had.

CHAPTER TEN

By nightfall, Brooke had her tattered emotions under control, but she was weakening, towards Mac. He'd come to her rescue. His kiss revealed he still wanted her, yet he'd shown his protectiveness when he'd held her after Duncan had left. And that was what she needed at the moment—a friend.

While she made coffee, Mac removed his leather jacket and thrown it over the back of the sofa. His leather pants hung on his slim hips, the black T-shirt he wore displayed every muscle on his magnificent body. Heavy motorbike boots covered his legs up to his calves.

As she handed him his mug, he flashed her that lopsided smile that made her go weak at the knees. *So much for me examining feelings later.* She led him to the small dining room table and took a seat. Yes, the more formal the better. She followed his lips as he blew on his coffee. *I'm pathetic. Oh, my Lord. I need to get him out of here before I beg him to kiss me again.*

"I think I should stay the night," Mac said.

Brooke was so busy watching his mouth like a hungry pup it took her a moment to take in what he'd said. She shook her head. "Oh no, Mac, there's no need for that, I'm sure Duncan won't bother me again."

The last thing she needed was Mac sleeping under her roof. That would lead to a situation she wasn't ready to face, no matter how much her body betrayed her. The ringing of her mobile dragged her wayward thoughts away from the man seated across from her.

She checked the caller ID before answering. "Hey, Tyrelle how was your day?"

"We had a great day, but Davey's upset so I'm going to bring him back to your place. I think I may have overdone it with the sweets. Do you mind if I stay as well?"

Brooke knew only too well how Davey could be if he wasn't feeling well. "Okay, of course you can stay. I'll see you both shortly."

That made things easier, there'd be no room for Mac to sleep. Feeling better, she pasted a smile on her lips, which made her feel like the damn Cheshire Cat.

"Tyrelle's bringing Davey home. He has a stomach ache so I won't be alone tonight. See, no need for you to stay." She smiled cheerfully.

"How far away does your friend live?"

Brooke eyed him warily. *Why would he want to know that?*

"About half an hour. Not that far, so you can go, I'll be okay until they get here."

He smiled as if he knew she was trying to get rid of him, which of course she was. Time alone with him was her enemy.

***

Mac watched the play of emotions dance across Brooke's features. He could guess where her thoughts had gone and suppressed a laugh, only because he'd been thinking the same thing.

Her slim hands shook on the coffee mug, her green eyes wide with apprehension. He leaned back in the chair and allowed his gaze to run over her face. He'd never get tired of watching her. A worried frown marred her beautiful features, she looked vulnerable, crushed. She shook her head and gazed at him.

"Your father told me about your younger brother dying. I'm sorry for your loss," Brooke said.

Feeling like a bucket of cold water had been thrown over him he stood, grabbed his coffee and stalked into the sitting room. He didn't want her pity. He stopped at the windows Brooke had looked out earlier. A brightly coloured shed stood under a large fig tree. He didn't realise she'd followed until she placed a hand on his shoulder.

"I'm sorry, Mac, I didn't mean to upset you."

"It's okay, I just didn't know Dad had spoken to you about Garry." Why hadn't his father said something? Warned him. He closed his eyes, fighting to control his emotions.

"Do you want to talk about it? Sometimes sharing one's loss can help us understand and accept."

Maybe she was right. If he could talk to anyone, it was Brooke. She wouldn't judge.

He drew in a deep breath. "After my mother died, Dad felt we needed to be part of a family. Maureen had been friends with my parents for years. Her husband had died in a car accident shortly after Mum. I guess they were both lonely. Their marriage wasn't a great love story. Not like Mum and Dad's, who'd been childhood sweethearts and always knew they'd end up together." He took a sip of his now cold coffee. "Garry was five years younger than me. I was so excited when he was born. Maureen was good to me, but I wasn't her son, not like Garry. I was just a kid who came along with the marriage."

Funny, growing up he'd thought they were a happy, loving family, but now he looked back on it, there was never much love in the house where Maureen was concerned. Not the way Brooke and Louise shared their love for Davey. Davey was never without a kiss or hug. He couldn't even remember Maureen giving Garry a hug, let alone him. Maureen lost interest in showing Garry off to her friends. Once he started losing his baby teeth, he was no longer the perfect child.

"Garry and I were close when we were younger. I was his big brother and looked out for him, made sure he didn't get into too much trouble. Trouble seemed to follow him around. When I went to uni, we lost touch. I'd come home for holidays, but Garry would be off somewhere with friends. We saw very little of each other."

He sensed rather than saw Brooke sit down. She didn't say a word, just let him talk.

"When I went into the family business with Dad, I stayed home for a while until I decided where I wanted to live. Garry and I seemed to find an even ground with each other, but I always had the feeling he was troubled. He had mood swings. One moment he was on top of the world, the next he'd drop into a deep depression. It wasn't until I came home from the office early one day and caught him snorting coke that I realized he needed help. He needed my help."

Hell, the pain he felt that day was still as strong as it had been when he'd seen his brother's glazed eyes. He still questioned why he hadn't picked up on the signs, they were all there.

"I convinced him to go into rehab. Maureen was devastated, blamed Dad and I for not knowing sooner. I thought he'd recovered. He even came into the family business."

He swallowed the lump in his throat and tightened his hold on the mug as if it was a lifeline.

"Three months ago I was heading over to Hong Kong on a business trip. I was walking out the door when Garry rang my mobile. He said he needed to talk to me, but I put him off, saying that the trip I was taking could make or break the deal we had worked so hard to get. He bloody-well begged me and I told him to grow up, that I'd be back in a couple of days and we'd talk then."

Please, Mac, I need to talk to you. I can't go on like this. The secret is eating me alive. Mac closed his eyes, fighting against the sound of Garry's pleading voice. He exhaled. "I received a call later that night telling me that Garry had died of an overdose."

Pain rocked his body, his shoulders hunched, and he let out the cry of grief that he had kept bottled up inside him since the phone call. The mug slipped from his fingers and splintered into pieces on the floor. Long shattered sobs vibrated through his body.

Warm arms wrapped around his shoulders. Brooke's soft murmurs of reassurance that he wasn't alone helped him come back from Hell. He dragged in a deep breath.

"If I'd just spoken to him, Garry would be here today."

She moved to stand in front of him and brushed a gentle hand over his forehead. "You don't know that. It sounds like your brother was a deeply troubled man. I believe that our path to death is ordained for us from when we were born. Garry's time had come, and at least now he no longer has the demons that obviously dominated his life." She brushed a kiss where her hands had been. "The thing you have to do is not let your guilt take over your life. I'm sure Garry wouldn't want you to do that."

He enclosed her in his arms and rested his cheek on top of her head. It felt good to have the warmth of her body close to him. It helped thaw the cold hand that clasped his heart.

They stood in each other's arms until headlights shone through the windows. Brooke took a step back and his arms fell to his side like heavy weights.

"The bathroom is at the top of the stairs. It will give you time to compose yourself before Davey sees you."

He kissed her cheek. "Thank you for listening."

In the bathroom, Mac splashed water over his face. He'd never felt so drained in all his life. He braced his arms on the basin and looked in the mirror. He was a wreck, but the pain that he'd carried around for the last three months felt lighter. Sharing with Brooke made him face the demon that had haunted him. He'd never get over the fact he might have been able to help Garry, but now he felt he could at least accept his brother's senseless death.

***

After cleaning up the broken coffee mug, Brooke opened the door for Tyrelle and Davey while Mac was upstairs. Davey had his head resting on her friend's shoulder. When he saw Brooke, he put his arms out to her.

"Hello, my precious boy."

Footsteps sounded on the stairs.

Davey's eyes widened and a large grin spread across his face. "Juzz Mac here, Roo," he said in a low voice.

"Yes, I know, sweetheart." Brooke smiled at her brother and dropped a kiss on the top of his head. "Did you have fun with Tyrelle?"

"Yep."

"That's good."

Brooke could see her friend's mind working as Mac walked towards them. Davey wiggled to get down then ran to Mac.

"Hi, little buddy."

He picked Davey up in one arm then extended the other to Tyrelle. "Hi, I'm Mac."

"Juzz Mac." Tyrelle smiled.

"Sorry, I'm rude," Brooke mumbled. "This is my friend, Tyrelle."

Her friend displayed a wide smile. "It's a pleasure to meet you, Juzz Mac. Davey's been talking about you all day."

Brooke closed her eyes and prayed her friend would not say something outrageous.

Tyrelle looked around at Mac's arse. "I can see why you get Brooke's motor running."

Please, Lord, just open the floor up now.

Mac glanced over at Brooke and laughed, sending heat to her face. "That's good to know, Tyrelle. I'll file that information for later."

"No need for information filing," Brooked said in a hurry. "It will do you no good. The motor has broken down."

She turned and went into the kitchen. *Bloody Tyrelle, I'm going to strangle her.*

***

Mac decided he liked Brooke's friend. She reminded him of a little pixie, dressed in a deep pink tutu style skirt with a light pink shoestring top and an assortment of bangles on both arms. The only thing out of place was the heavy army boots she wore over pink and purple stockings.

Mac sat on the lounge, tucking Davey into his side. "Tell me a bit about yourself, Tyrelle."

"Oh, not a lot to tell really. I'm a gay truck driver on holidays at the moment."

"A truck driver?" That was the last thing he expected. *How the hell did someone that tiny manage to handle a vehicle that size?*

"I'm stronger than I look." Tyrelle swung a leg as she perched on the arm of a seat. "You didn't blink when I said I was gay."

Mac gathered that Brooke's friend wasn't accepted by many because of her sexual preference. "Should I have? I have friends who are gay, so it's not something that bothers me. You seem to be a good friend to Brooke and Davey, that's what matters to me."

"Right, I think we'll get along just fine, Juzz Mac." She stood and sauntered into the kitchen with Brooke.

Davey, who'd been sitting quietly while he and

Tyrelle talked, now wanted Mac's undivided attention.

***

Brooke was adding the final touches to the salad she'd prepared for her dinner earlier with a few more ingredients so there would be enough for everyone. She glared when Tyrelle walked into the kitchen.

"You had sex with him, didn't you? Please say you did." Her friend leaned a hip against the cupboard. Her face lit with excitement.

"No, we didn't have sex."

"Damn, even I'm tempted to change to the dark side."

Brooke laughed and shook her head. "You're hopeless, my friend. Do you want to set the table?"

"Sure, it's not like I'm going to get any juicy information out of you."

It was going to be so hard to sit around the table having a meal and making small talk. She felt like she and Mac had become friends tonight, not just two people physically attracted to each other, but she needed time to re-examine her feelings. Could she get past the lies and try again? She closed her eyes and prayed that whatever her decision, no one would get hurt—especially Davey.

After dinner, Brooke put Davey to bed and read him a story. She kissed the top of his head. "I love you, baby."

"Davey love you too, Roo."

Mac and her friend were deep in a conversation

and having a coffee when she came down the stairs.

"Mac was just telling me about his bike collection." Tyrelle's eyes widened with enthusiasm. "He has a 1940 WLDR."

"Wow, how thrilling." Brooke lowered herself into her favourite lounge chair and pulled her legs up under her bottom. A coffee waited on the table beside her.

"You don't even know what a WLDR is," her friend said.

"True." Brooke shrugged. "But you're excited so it must be good."

Mac chuckled, but made no comment.

She took a sip of her coffee and glanced over the lip of the mug. "So, Mac, you'll be able to go home once you finish your coffee."

"Trying to get rid of me, princess?"

That bloody grin of his, he darn well knows what it does to me. "No, no. It's just that the roads can be quite traitorous at night."

He laughed. "I think I can manage, but if you're sure you'll be right, I'll leave you and Tyrelle so you can get an early night."

He stood, placing his coffee mug on the low table in front of the lounge. Brooke unwound herself from her seat and walked him to the door.

"Well, thanks for your help this afternoon. I really appreciate you coming out."

He ran his fingers down her cheek, his eyes turning a deeper blue. A shiver raced down her spine.

She had to force herself not to lean forward and kiss his delectable mouth.

"Not a problem, princess," he whispered then he turned and left.

She brushed the back of her hand over the spot where his fingers had touched. *Lord, I'm going to end up in the loony bin if I keep this up.*

***

Mac strode away from Brooke's with an uneasy feeling in his gut. However, short of bullying Brooke into letting him stay, there was little he could do. She was probably right. Surely, Duncan wouldn't do anything else tonight.

A white van with headlights on high beam careered around the corner, almost collecting Mac. He had to jump out of the way, falling to the ground just in time as it sped past. With his arms resting on his knees, he dragged in a few deep breaths.

Gazing down towards Brooke's house, he saw the brake lights of the van come on and realised it was at the side of the property. Then a flash of light flew through the air.

Bloody hell.

Jumping to his feet he ran back towards Brooke's as the van roared past him again. All he could see were two dark figures in the front. The number plate was covered in mud. *Bastards!*

Heart pounding, he raced up the steps and hammered on the door.

Tyrelle opened it, fear etched on her face. "Thank

God! Someone fire-bombed Brooke's studio!"

"Where?"

"Out the back. Brooke went out there to check on something. I've called the emergency services."

Mac brushed past Tyrelle and raced through the open sliding door. Fear growing with each step. *No, no, don't let anyone else die because I wasn't there to protect them.*

"Brooke!"

Brooke lay on the ground outside the studio not moving. A cold sweat broke out over his entire body. *God no, God no!*

He carefully scooped Brooke into his arms to move her away from the fire. "Princess, can you hear me?" he pleaded.

Mac sank to the ground, holding her close. The bright orange flicker from the blaze gave him enough light to run his gaze over Brooke to check she was okay. He couldn't see that she had sustained any injuries, but the paramedics would be here soon to check her out. One thing was clear—he sure as hell wasn't leaving them here tonight.

"Mac?" She opened her eyes and lifted a shaky hand to her head.

"I'm here. I should never have left." Guilt and fear rocked him.

She gazed towards the burning building and struggled to get out of his arms.

"The painting of Mum and Davey."

"We can't go in there, princess. There's nothing to

save."

Heart-wrenching sobs raked her body. She buried her face into his shoulder. He kissed her forehead and held her closer. The sirens from fire engines rose in the distance. The fuel inside the studio fed the flames into a raging, angry inferno.

Firefighters raced to the cottage and attacked the building with jet power hoses.

"Anyone in there?" One of the firefighters asked as he came to stand beside them.

"No, thank God."

Two paramedics hurried across the yard to where Mac sat with Brooke. They ran through a series of tests and asked Brooke name, date of birth and address to make sure she was coherent.

"Where you in the shed when it went up, Miss Fairfax?" The firefighter who'd introduced himself as John asked.

"No, I was going back to the house after checking the studio was locked up. I got knocked to the ground by the explosion," Brooke whispered her response.

"Well, we'll get you to the hospital and get you examined properly."

"No," she replied with determination, even though her voice was weak.

"Miss Fairfax."

"I'll call the doctor once we get back to Bindarra Creek," Mac interjected.

With the reassurance that Brooke would receive medical attention, the paramedics left.

Mac carried Brooke up to where Tyrelle stood on the back porch her arms wrapped around her slim figure. Tears stained her cheeks.

"Is she okay?"

Brooke was shaking uncontrollably against his chest.

"Shock is setting in. Let's get her inside."

They walked into the sitting room. Mac sat on the sofa holding Brooke on his lap.

Tyrelle returned and handed him a tumbler of water.

"Drink this, princess." He placed the glass to her lips, encouraging her to take a sip. "Is Davey all right?"

"Yes, he's still asleep. I checked on him a few minutes ago. Slept through the whole thing," Tyrelle replied, holding a glass filled with a richly-coloured liquid that looked like brandy or whiskey.

"Drink your brandy, it's been a stressful night," Mac told Brooke's friend.

"Thank God you came back." Tyrelle took a long drink from her glass.

"I should never have left in the first place," he bit out. His gaze ran over Brooke's tear-stained face.

"Looks like the fire is almost out," Tyrelle said. "Did you want a brandy? I didn't think to ask."

"No, I'll need to drive you all back to Bindarra Creek."

Brooke's mobile beeped a message. Mac picked it up from the table. Red-hot fury jolted through his body when he read the message.

This was a warning.

"The bastards."

Brooke lifted her head from his shoulder. She looked like a frightened kitten. At least, she'd stopped shaking. Moving from his lap, she sat beside him.

"Try to drink some more water." She nodded and took a sip from the glass.

***

A knock at the door made Brooke jump. Mac left her on the sofa and went to answer the door. She felt lost without his arms around her.

"I'm Constable Stephen Wright, and this is Constable Len Wills," a deep voice came from the doorway. "We've been sent to talk to the owner about the fire."

"Come in, officers," she heard Mac reply.

Brooke related the events of the afternoon and Duncan's threats. Mac showed the constables the text message Brooke had received.

"Can you identify this number?"

Brooke checked the number. "It's my brother's business phone."

She had gone beyond fear. Now she had rage building to the point that if her brother walked into the room right now, she would throttle him.

"A bit clumsy of him to use one of his own phones."

"He's not the sharpest tool in the shed," Mac responded.

Brooke had to agree.

After giving them Brooke's and his mobile numbers, Mac saw the officers out then came to sit beside her again, taking her hand and lifting it to his lips.

"Pack some clothes and I'll drive you all back to Bindarra Creek."

Would Duncan be stupid enough to go after their mother? Brooke worried and was relieved she had organised security for the estate.

Placing the glass of water on the table, she headed for the stairs so she could have a shower and collect her and Davey's bags.

"I'll just go home," Tyrelle said.

"No, I want you to come with us, Tyrelle." Brooke turned with her hand on the bannister. "I don't know what Duncan might do next."

"We'll call past your place on our way out," Mac said. "I'll ring your mother, Brooke, and tell her we're on our way back to town. Is it okay to take your car, Tyrelle?"

"Sure."

"I'll get my bike and move it into your garage with your car, Brooke. Where are the keys?" Mac asked.

"On the stand by the door."

Brooke packed a few clothes then went in to wake Davey. He was a little grizzly to be woken up out of his sleep, but he'd soon dozed off again once they were on their way.

The drive back to Bindarra Creek was a silent one.

Brooke sat in the back, Davey sleeping in her arms. She gazed out the window into the darkness that surrounded them. It felt much like heart—an empty wasteland.

Were Father and Candice part of the plot? She was unsure of her father, but hoped Candice knew nothing about the fire.

The gates opened as they turned the corner to the front of the estate. Stewart was waiting at the gates and waved them through. A white security van was parked out the front of the house. After Mac had pulled up, he came around and lifted Davey from the car.

Her mother ran down the steps, pulling Brooke into her embrace. "Darling, what happened? Mac said there was a fire."

Brooke stepped back and said, "If you go with Mac and get Davey settled, I'll ask Ellen to make some coffee. It's going to take some time to explain things, Mum."

"Tyrelle, can you ask Mathew to call Doctor Warner to come out to check on Brooke, please?" Mac asked.

"I'm—"

"No, Mac's right, darling."

"Alright, if it will put your mind at rest, Mum," Brooke said.

Brooke watched her mother and Mac take Davey into the house. Mathew and Ellen appeared in the doorway.

She ran up the stairs into Ellen's open arms and allowed the woman to lead her into the house. "*Caro*, we've been so worried."

"I know, Mac and I will explain when Mum comes down." Brooke gave the couple a reassuring smile. "Could you make some tea and coffee, please?"

"Of course, it is on," Ellen replied and squeezed Brooke's hand.

"The luggage is in the foyer, Brooke," Stewart said.

She turned to her friends and replied, "Thanks."

Mac and her mother entered the room. Her mother's face white, her breathing shallow.

"Mum?" Brooke raced over, grabbed her mother's arm and led her to the sofa. "Come and sit down."

"Are you okay, Mrs Fairfax?" Tyrelle asked.

"Just a bit of shock," her mother replied. "Brooke, please sit and tell me what happened."

Brooke sat next to her mother with Mac next to Brooke, holding her hand. Stewart and Tyrelle each sat in the single seats.

She sent Mac a pleading glance. She didn't think she'd be able to explain to her mother without breaking down. Ellen and Mathew returned with the coffee and tea then sat on the other sofa, waiting Mac to speak.

***

Resting his forearms on his knees, Mac idly rubbed his thumb over Brooke's knuckles as he explained the events of the day, starting with the conversation he'd overheard between the two Fairfax men. He tried to maintain a calm and neutral voice as he relayed the exchange between Brooke and Duncan. He kept a close eye on Brooke and her mother, ready to stop if Louise showed any sign of the information being overly taxing.

Periodically, she or Stewart would ask a question and he answered as best he could.

"So, what comes next?" Louise asked.

"The police will more than likely arrest Duncan for arson and he will have to appear in court. I'm not overly sure of the procedure, we'll have to wait and see," Mac replied with a shrug.

The doorbell rang and Mathew went to answer it. A short while later he returned with Doctor Hill following closely behind him.

"Karen, thank you for coming out so late." Louise stood then swayed slightly on her feet. Mac jumped up and grabbed hold of her arm to steady her.

"I think it might be best if I take a look at you first, Louise," Karen said.

"Stewart, could you help Mac take Mum to her room?" Brooke asked. "Mum, I think it would be best if you go to bed after Karen is finished."

"I agree," Karen said as she followed the group up the stairs.

A few minutes later, Mac and Stewart headed back down the stairs. "What sort of security have you installed here so far?" Mac asked.

Stewart explained what procedures he had taken and what he still had to install the next day. Satisfied with what was in place, Mac walked into the sitting room to find Tyrelle, Mathew and Ellen talking.

"How are you doing, Tyrelle?" he said.

"I'm fine. I'm just a bit worried about Brooke."

"Yes, this is why she needs the doctor to have a look at her. Do you mind if I borrow your car? I'll bring it back tomorrow after picking up Brooke's car and my bike."

"Sure, bring it back anytime, I won't be going anywhere for a few days. The keys are still in it."

Stewart handed him a code for the gate. "If you're going to be in and out, you best have one of these."

Mac accepted with a nod.

Brooke stepped into the sitting room looking worn out, a tired smile on her face. "You will be pleased to know I am okay. No side effects from tonight's adventure."

"And your mum?" Mac asked.

"Good, but she needs to cut down her stress levels. Unfortunately, I don't think that will happen for a while."

"Thank you for setting up the security, Stew." Brooke walked over, kissed his cheek and accepted his hug. Brooke held onto him tightly. "I love you so much."

"Love you too, sweets."

Mac felt the need to punch someone and that someone was Stewart, the security guy. His gut tightened at the thought of Brooke with this guy. *What the hell was she doing kissing me if she's in a relationship with Mr Stewart-Freaking-Wonderful?*

The sight of Brooke in the arms of another man knocked him for a six.

Who did he have to blame? No one except himself, that's who. He'd known all along women were lying cheats. Hadn't Larissa proven that to him? For a while, he'd thought Brooke was different, but from the look of things, she was tarred with the same brush as every other woman he knew from cashed-up families.

"I need to go," he said abruptly.

"Mac, Mum asked if she could speak to you before you go," Brooke said. "Her sitting room is upstairs to the left."

"Sure." He couldn't say no to a request from Louise. He took the steps two at a time. The sooner he got this over with, the sooner he could leave.

The room he entered was very feminine. Two peach-coloured sofas were arranged to face each other with a low white coffee table in between. Photos of the Fairfax children decorated a white wall and on the opposite one was a large abstract painting in pastel colours. Mac knew the moment he saw it that it was one Brooke had painted. Just like the one in Davey's room was one of Brooke's works.

"Mac, thank you for coming up. Have a seat." When he'd taken the seat across from her Louise said, "There are a few things I'd like to discuss with you. Brooke told me about your identity. Why all the secrecy?"

"I'm not sure if I can explain it to you, Louise."

"Try, nonetheless," she said. She had the same determination in her eyes that he'd seen in Brooke's eyes from time to time. "I felt the other night that your father was an honest man, yet you both deceived us."

"Louise, this has nothing to do with my father."

Mac stood and paced the room. "Dad probably told you that my younger brother died a few months back. I felt responsible, so I left Sydney to come to terms with my grief and guilt. Dad had no idea I was here until the night Davey went missing."

"Oh, Mac, I'm sorry." Louise stood and took his hand in hers. "I can't imagine what it must be like for you."

He walked away from her to look at the photos on the wall.

He glanced over his shoulder towards Louise. "Why does any of this matter to you?"

"If we're to do business with your firm, I need to know that we can trust you," she said simply. "Brooke no doubt told you that she is the trustee of Ingalls Development. With my husband and other children now out of the business, Brooke feels it would be best for the time being that she and I run it together."

Mac turned to watch her, surprised by the force of her words. The gossip around town was that Louise Fairfax lived under her husband's thumb and had no business sense.

"No, she didn't, but I got that impression from a

conversation I overheard between your son and husband."

This issue could cause all sorts of problems for his father and him. If Brooke and Louise didn't know what they were doing, the whole project could go to the wall. It might be easier just to pull out altogether.

"Let me explain our situation. Gordon took on the role as manager of the company when my father became ill, but Dad still had the final say on any project. For Gordon's part, he received a generous salary for his position as well as taking a percentage of the profits," she said with a tight smile. "Until now there has been no cause to inform him or my other children about Brooke's position in the company. As you know, things changed recently."

"Pardon me for asking, but just how viable is the business?"

"The business is solid, Mac. If you've done a background check, you must know that."

"Gordon could also take you to court for the company."

"He can try, but the will is legal. Dad was of sound mind when it was drawn up. Any other claim Gordon may feel he has to my personal assets will come to nothing, he signed a prenup. I have a very good lawyer, Mac, and my assets are secure. If you're concerned about my business ability, will it help if I tell you that I ran the company with Dad from behind the scenes? I have a diploma in business and finance. My illness is the only reason Gordon took over the reins completely. I had no reason to suspect he would do anything that might jeopardise Ingalls Development."

"Why did your father feel the need to make Brooke trustee and not you?"

"Dad trusted Brooke to do what was best for the family as a whole. She is extremely bright and picks up things easily. Duncan has his problems with alcohol and, as I've recently discovered, drugs too. Candice does whatever her father tells her. It's one thing to let Gordon have control in the short-term, quite another for him to hold the reins in the long-term."

Mac looked down at the floor. The image of Brooke wrapped in another man's arms burned in his gut. *Great, just what I need—daily contact with Brooke.* He could feel Louise's eyes on him but continued to take great interest in his shoes.

"Mac, do you have a problem working with women?"

He lifted his eyes. "No, not at all, Louise. I have a lot of respect for you."

"But not for my daughter?"

"I didn't say that."

"No, you didn't. Mac, give her a chance, she hasn't had an easy time with her father and siblings. My father was the one who saw Brooke's true potential. He was the only man she ever trusted completely."

Mac didn't know what to say to that, so he held his tongue.

"I expect you'll need to call your father and discuss this turn of events," Louise said.

"Yes, I'll call him when I get home. It'll probably take a couple of days before Dad can return. Would Thursday suit?"

"Yes. Eleven o'clock Thursday."

"I'll let Dad know. Sleep well, Louise."

***

Brooke waited for Mac at the foot of the stairs. She felt like a schoolgirl waiting for her first love. The fire had made her aware how very short life could be, and she wanted to spend as much time with Mac as possible. She'd had time to re-examine her feelings for Mac. Yes, he'd deceived her, but he hadn't done it out of malice. She understood now his need for solitude. If word got out about his brother's drug addiction, the tabloids would have been out for blood. Stafford and Sons was a big enough company to draw that sort of attention.

When Mac descended the stairs, he didn't look very happy. He ran his fingers through his hair, something he did whenever he seemed stressed. A shiver of unease slid down her spine.

"Is everything okay?" she asked as he stepped into the foyer.

He glared down at her. "Yeah, things are just hunky dory. We have a meeting on Thursday at eleven in the morning to get this mess over the project sorted."

Taken aback by the cold, abrupt answer, Brooke

went on the attack. "That should work. We'll expect to see you then!" She turned to leave, but stopped herself. "I think it would be best to keep our relationship as purely business."

Her heart ached and her stomach knotted.

"I couldn't agree more," he replied in a flat voice.

Feeling like he'd taken a knife to her chest, she left him standing in the foyer and made her way upstairs to her room. Slamming the door shut, she threw herself down on her bed and cried like she'd never cried before. For the first time in her life, she knew what it felt like to have a broken heart, and it sucked.

How she would be able to work with him day after day, she didn't know. Nevertheless, she would do it. She'd do it to prove to him that she could. That he was not the beginning and the end of her existence. She would work with him to prove to herself that she didn't need him to be able to breathe.

CHAPTER ELEVEN

On Wednesday morning, Brooke was sitting at the breakfast bar chatting with Tyrelle and Davey when Mathew handed her the morning paper.

"Not good news, Miss Brooke." He walked away, shaking his head.

Fairfax Family Embroiled in another Scandal, the title read.

Bloody great! The way things were going Roland and Mac wouldn't want to go in with the subdivision deal. Could Ingalls afford to go it alone?

Brooke sighed and picked up a piece of toast, continuing to read.

Duncan Fairfax, son of Property Developer Gordon Fairfax, was arrested yesterday and charged with arson for the fire-bombing of his sister Brooke Fairfax's art studio.

Ms Fairfax was reportedly caught up in another altercation on Friday night after being assaulted. There has been no comment on either incidence from the Fairfax family.

"Not good?" her friend asked.

"No." Brooke passed her friend the paper. Tyrelle whistled.

Brooke spent most of the day with Davey and Tyrelle, taking Davey out to Bellevue Stables for a pony ride before stopping in at Beth's for an ice cream. Brooke hadn't seen Mac since the night of the fire. Beth told her that Fred had helped Mac with retrieving her car and Mac's bike. Brooke had been with her mother while Mac had been busy running around with returning her car and Tyrelle's four-wheel. Not that she wanted to see him anyway. Theirs was just a business relationship now. She couldn't help that her heart gave a jolt when she looked across at Fred's garage, hoping to catch a glimpse of Mac.

On Thursday morning, Davey declared he wanted to see the ducks down in the pond at the back of the house while they ate breakfast.

Tyrelle stood and held her hand out to Davey. "Well, come along, man. Let's get some bread from Ellen." She glanced at Brooke and smiled. "I'll keep him occupied until after your meeting. When he gets tired of the ducks, we'll take the back stairs to his room."

Brooke stood and gave her friend a tight hug. "Thank you, I'll have Ellen make you both something for morning tea."

Dressed in a plain green dress and high-heeled pumps, Brooke felt ready to face the day of business.

After Tyrelle and Davey had left, Brooke couldn't sit still. She wished she'd had her paints with her then she could have thrown paint on a canvas and let out her frustration. Of course, she wasn't even sure if Mac was going to turn up. He could still be playing mechanic, for all she knew.

Their family lawyer, Clarence Lansky greeted her

with a warm smile as she entered the sitting room where he sat talking with her mother. Clarence always struck Brooke as a reserved man, ready for business and with little time for small talk. His handlebar moustache seemed out of place with his business dress style.

When she heard knocking Brooke left her mother and Clarence still in discussion to answer the door. Roland stood on the doorstep alone. She forced herself not to look to see if Mac was out by the car.

"Good morning, Roland," she greeted.

"Hello, Brooke dear."

"Mum is in the sitting room. We thought we'd have the meeting in there rather than Father's office. It still has the smell of lingering cigar." She wrinkled her nose.

Roland nodded his agreement. "Brit should be here soon. He had a couple of things to do first, and I believe our lawyers will be arriving around noon."

Brooke let out a sigh of relief as she led him into the sitting room. Her mother hurriedly slipped some papers into a folder. Brooke sent her a questioning glance.

Her mother rose to greet Roland. "Roland, it's lovely to see you again."

"Likewise, Louise."

"Let me introduce our solicitor, Clarence Lansky. Clarence, Roland Stafford."

"Roland, would you mind if I spoke to Mum privately for a moment?"

Mathew entered, carrying a tray of refreshments.

Roland smiled. "Of course not. I'll enjoy a coffee while I wait."

Clarence left the room with Mathew, leaving Roland by himself. Brooke frowned when her mother picked up the folder before following her into the office. "What's up, Mum?"

"It looks like your father has been embezzling money from one of the accounts. Raymond rang while you answered the door."

The bloody bastard. "How much?"

"He's not sure until he's examined all the accounts."

"What's in the folder?"

"It's a receipt from Seb Peacock for the land your father purchased for the subdivision."

Brooke furrowed her brows. "Why would Father have that here? Shouldn't that be held at the office?"

Her mother's hands shook as she handed the paper over to her. She explained how she'd been searching the study for a document for Clarence and came across the receipt.

Brooke looked at the paper. "Holy hell! Mr Peacock's land is worth twice this amount." She glanced up at her mother.

"I agree," said her mother. "We'll go and speak to Seb at the nursing home and find out if he was enticed to sell the land below its value. If need be, we'll reimburse him any money we believe would meet the market price."

"That sounds fair."

After placing the folder on the desk to read the contents in more detail later, Brooke and her mother left the office. *I knew this was going to be an appalling day.*

The doorbell rang again. This time Brooke left it to Mathew to answer. When he showed Mac into the room, Brooke's heart leaped into her throat. His hair was now combed into a more formal style although the long dark locks still brushed against his collar, he carried himself like a man used to handling business. This was Mac Stafford, the businessman. His dark suit emphasised his wide shoulders.

Their eyes connected and held. For a split second it was as if they were the only two people in the room. Then one of them blinked, and Brooke hoped it was her.

"Brit, finally I have my boy back," Roland said as he gave his son a bear hug. The affection these two men had for each other was undeniable. Mac patted his father's back.

"Dad, I'm not so sure about the boy thing." Mac laughed. His gaze returned to Brooke.

What did he want from her? She had nothing to give him. She felt emotionally drained. "I think it's time we got this underway," Brooke said, wanting to put an end to this meeting as soon as possible.

"Before we start, I think it's best if I inform you what we discovered this morning." Her mother licked her lips. "It seems Gordon may have embezzled money from Ingalls. We're not sure on the exact amount yet. Our accountant is investigating it for us."

"You said on Monday night the business was sound," Mac stated, glancing between Brooke and her mother.

Was he accusing her mother of lying? Brooke fisted her hands. Her mother placed a hand on her knee. She glared from father to son. Mac stared back with what Brooke viewed as distrust in his eyes.

Who was he not to trust her? She had been honest with him all along. He was the one with all the secrets, the bloody mutton-head. She ignored the fact that she'd understood his reason on Monday night.

"Mac, I'm sure it's not a big problem," Roland started.

"Your son seems to think otherwise, Roland," Brooke bit out.

"Brooke, settle down. You've taken us by surprise, that's all," Mac told her.

"Well why were you looking at my mother as if she was some criminal?" she flared at him. She stood, digging her fingernails into her palm and grinding her teeth.

"I was not looking at your mother like that at all." Mac stalked over to her.

She poked him in the chest. "Yes, you were. When you questioned what Mum had said on Monday night, you looked at her like she was dirt under your feet."

"I happen to think a lot of your mother. She is one of the few women I know who is upfront and honest," he barked back.

"Not like me, you mean?" Brooke took a step closer to him. "Let me remind you that it was you who lied. You're the one who kept your identity a secret."

"Well, at least, I didn't make moves on someone else while still in a relationship." His face was mere inches from hers now. His eyes had turned midnight blue.

She shook her head. *Relationship? Who was in a relationship?*

"What the hell are you babbling about now?"

"You and Mr Wonderful Security Man."

Brooke stared at Mac, dumbfounded for a moment then laughed.

"You thought Stewart and I were together?" She laughed again. "You are so wrong."

"Okay, children, that's enough," Roland said, sending his son a warning glance. "Let's get down to business, Ross will be here soon."

Brooke sat down next to her mother again, but every time she looked at Mac she got the giggles again. He looked back at her with stony eyes, which only had her laughing more.

"Brooke, please," her mother chastised her.

"Okay ... I'm fine now." She hiccupped.

Mac gave her a thunderous stare, then stood and grabbed her hand, pulling her to her feet.

"We'll be back shortly," he said, tugging her along with him.

"I don't want to go with you, you overgrown ox."

"Too bad, you're coming."

He pushed open the first door he came to and dragged Brooke inside, shutting it behind him. His nostrils flared, as he stared down at her.

This is not good.

One minute he was staring at her with disdain, the next he had her in his arms devouring her mouth, her neck and back to her mouth.

"You will be the death of me," he said between kisses.

"Stop, we're not going there." She pulled her head back.

He drew her back into his arms and trailed kisses down her neck. Her nipples beaded as he ran a hand over her breast.

"No." Brooke pushed against his chest and backed away from him. "Don't ever do that again."

She turned to leave the room, but the coolness in his voice stopped her.

"You say no, but your body is screaming yes. I could take you on this desk and you wouldn't stop me."

She turned and stared at him coldly. "But I'm still saying no. You can talk all you want, kiss me into submission, but I've still said no."

Mac's face paled, his hands clasped into fists.

"Mac, I'm—"

Eyes like slates of blue ice bored into her before he stormed from the room and slammed the door behind him.

Brooke dropped her face into her hands. *Shit, shit, shit.*

***

Mac stalked through the foyer and out the front door, slamming it for good measure. He stood on the veranda, dragging in deep long breaths. Never had any woman made him lose his temper like Brooke had. He could go from wanting to kiss her senseless to wanting to strangle her in a matter of minutes. Brooke invoked a flame that seemed to consume his soul.

He walked down the steps, and with his hands in his pockets, paced the front of the house. Her words thundered in his head. Was it arrogance that made him say what he had? He knew beyond all doubt that she responded to him just as much as he did to her, but he would never push her beyond the point if she said no.

He stopped and looked up at the sky. How would their respective companies be able to work together while this underlying tension lingered between him and Brooke?

Dad and Louise will have to handle the details of the project.

And he'd forgotten to ask her about the bloody security guy. *Damn.* He ran a hand through his hair. So much for acting professionally.

***

Brooke entered the sitting room to find her

mother and Roland sitting on one of the sofas, talking in hushed tones. They glanced at her, concern in their eyes.

She plopped down on the sofa in an undignified manner and said, "Your son is a giant pain in the bum, Roland."

God, when will my life ever be sane again? She looked up at the ceiling. She would have to apologise to Mac. The accusation she'd thrown at him was disgusting. Mac was not the type of man who would ever force himself on a woman.

Mac entered the room, his hair no longer tidy. Brooke chewed her bottom lip. He didn't look at her, his face still tight with anger. He took off his suit jacket and flung it over the back of the sofa before rolling up his shirtsleeves.

She stood, wanting to go over and apologise for her behavior.

Mathew came into the room and announced that Candice had arrived.

"It might be best to postpone the rest of the meeting," Roland said.

"No," Brooke told them. "Let's get this all sorted today. I don't want it left up in the air."

"Dad, I think Brooke is right. We need to have our plans settled so we all know what we're dealing with."

Roland said, "If that is how you want to play it. Maybe we should wait in another room."

"No. Roland, Mac knows the history of my dealings

with my family. I'd feel better if you and he stayed," Brooke responded.

"If that is what you would like, Brooke," Roland said, giving her a reassuring smile.

"It is." She didn't look at Mac. She knew if she did she would fall apart.

Her sister hesitated in the doorway and glanced around the room. It was the first time Brooke had ever seen Candice unsure of herself.

Candice bit her lip. Clearing her throat, she said, "I was hoping I could have a word with you and Mum in private, Brooke."

Brooke sat back down on the sofa. "Whatever you have to say can be said in front of Roland and Mac."

Candice's gaze flickered between the two men before she nodded her acceptance of the situation. She walked into the room, her movements jerky. As Candice took one of the single seats, Brooke watched her with a twinge of regret that things weren't different between them.

"I want to say that I had no idea Duncan intended to cause you harm, Brooke," Candice said, pleading for Brooke to understand.

"That's easy for you to say now, Miss Fairfax," Mac said.

Brooke glanced over at him and could see he was only barely holding his anger in check.

Candice jerked her head towards Mac. "I...I know, but I promise on Grandpa's grave, I knew nothing of Duncan's plans."

Her sister's hand shook as she fumbled for a tissue from her bag.

"Daddy told me that Duncan was going to talk to you, to make you see reason with this business deal." She wiped tears from her cheeks. Brooke didn't even know Candice knew how to cry. "We've put a lot of work into this project over the last six months and we didn't want to lose it."

"Do you think Father knew what Duncan had planned?"

Candice shrugged. "I don't know. He didn't come back to my apartment last night. I only found out about the fire this morning when I read the newspaper. I promise you, Brooke, I meant you no physical harm."

"You made some incriminating threats towards your sister the other day, Candice," her mother said. Her lips were white with obvious distress.

"I ... know, but I could never intentionally hurt someone, especially not my family." Candice dropped her eyes to her lap.

Brooke glanced at her sister. "How much do you know about Father's embezzlement?"

Her sister raised her head with a jerk her eyes wide. "Nothing! Why would Daddy need to embezzle money from the company? He was receiving a more than generous return for his position."

Brooke believed Candice. Not even Candice was that good an actress. "The locks have been changed on the Ingalls offices, as you probably know by now.

The staff have been given time off with full pay until we settle this mess concerning Father."

"What am I to do?"

"I don't know yet, Candice. Mum and I will have to talk about it with Roland and Mac. If this subdivision goes ahead, this affects them as much as us. In the meantime, have a holiday. It might do you good."

Candice stood, looking almost deflated. "I'm sorry, Mother, I meant you no harm, but Daddy can be very persuasive, not that it's an excuse for the way I've treated you both."

Louise opened her arms to her eldest daughter and Candice rushed across the room. Brooke fought back the tears. *Maybe some good will come out of all this crap.*

"I'll leave you to your business," Candice said and ran from the room.

***

Mac contemplated the events that had transpired and hoped for Brooke's sake a relationship between the sisters could be achieved.

Mathew announced the arrival of Mac's lawyer, Ross Hampton, who was followed by an older man Mac assumed to be Brooke's lawyer.

Ross was a man in his early thirties with the blond good looks of a surfer. Mac often asked him why he chose to become a lawyer, but never received a direct answer.

With introductions made, everyone took their seats around the coffee table. Both men opened their briefcases.

"Well, let's get some of this worked out then we can always continue tomorrow if there is a need for another appointment."

For an hour, they hashed out the workings of the business model. The original plan for the housing subdivision would go ahead, but the added proposal for a shopping complex was shelved indefinitely. An account for the project would be opened at the local bank, which Mac and Brooke would handle. As the original proposal was between Ingalls Development and Stafford & Sons, there would be no grounds for Brooke's father to partition the courts.

Ross said, "As he approached you on behalf of Ingalls Development and with his position now terminated, he no longer has any say in the matter."

Roland stood and paced the room. Mac knew this was not a good sign.

"Perhaps we should form a separate business for the project. A joint business partnership," Roland said.

"Oh, Roland, that is a fabulous idea," Louise replied. It was the first smile Mac had seen on Louise's face for hours.

"Good, good," Clarence said. "Ross and I will draw up the paperwork and you two youngsters can come and see us sometime tomorrow. That work for you, Ross?"

"Fine by me," Ross replied.

A time for the meeting to be held at Clarence's

office was arranged.

"No ... I don't think that's a good idea," Brooke stammered.

"I thought it might be a good idea for you and Louise to work on this, Dad," Mac suggested.

Four sets of eyes turned towards Mac and Brooke. Heat flushed up over Brooke's face, making her look adorable. *Business, this is about business*.

"No, you and Brooke can handle this. What do you think, Louise?" Roland interjected.

With the details finally settled, everyone stood ready to leave. The doorbell rang and Brooke ran from the room.

"Brooke, my darling," the deep voice carried through to where the rest of them stood.

Mac wondered who'd arrived and was talking to Brooke in such an affectionate way. He walked out to the foyer at a steady pace.

Not again! Brooke had some moron hugging her. *For God's sake, how many men did she have on a leash?*

"Rupert, what the hell is the matter with you?" Brooke pulled away, but wasn't out of his arms for long before he was gathering her to him again.

"My sweetling, I was so worried about you."

Brooke struggled against the other man's hold.

"Buddy, I think she wants you to let her go," Mac said between clenched teeth.

"Mac, I'm quite capable of handling Rupert."

"Seems you're capable of handling a lot of men all

at once," Mac bit back.

Rupert let her go and stood back, looking Mac up and down. "Sweetheart, have you been holding out on me."

The man eyed Mac as if he'd like to eat him.

"Down boy, he's not interested in you," Brooke said, grinning.

"Are you sure?"

"Yes, Rupert, I'm sure, and if Stewart catches you eyeing off another man, he'll have your testicles for dinner."

It was then he realised Rupert was gay. He felt like a fool. He was a fool for letting his imagination run away with him and what he'd first believed of Brooke.

Mac looked between Brooke and Rupert. Stewart, the security man, was gay. *No bloody way.*
He felt the weight lift from his chest, until he realised he'd made some dreadful accusations towards Brooke and she might not forgive him too quickly. She stood in front of him with a smirk on those gorgeous lips, her arms folded across her breasts and one foot tapped on the marble floor. If she thought he would apologise in front of everyone, she could think again. That would not happen.

"I'll see you tomorrow at ten," he said abruptly before fleeing. He'd find another way to show her he was sorry.

CHAPTER TWELVE

Brooke lay in bed that night wondering how things would pan out. Would she and Mac be able to work together? And how would she be able to keep her true feelings for him a secret, when every time she saw him she wanted to be in his arms?

Her mind filtered over the events of the last couple of days. On Monday when he'd come to her house ready to protect her from Duncan, he'd shown that he cared a little about her, at least. He'd shown signs of jealousy over Stewart and Rupert.

Was it possible he cared for her more than he was letting her believe? Was she brave enough to take that chance? And what would be the best way to get him to love her as much as she loved him?

She went to sleep thinking about the way he'd

kissed her like a fragile flower before passion overtook them both. The more she thought about it, the more she was sure that Mac Stafford loved her. He just didn't know it yet.

I'll just have to show him.

***

Mac prowled his small apartment, unable to sleep. Brooke and her luscious body were on his mind, and it didn't seem to matter what he did, there was no way for him to suppress his thoughts. He grabbed the keys to his bike. A ride would be his best chance to get her out of his head. Before he knew where he was, he was pulling up in front of the Ingalls Estate. Taking his helmet off, he ran his hands through his hair. He sat on his bike trying to decide what he should do.

What would be the best way to handle Brooke? She responded to him so freely, but was that all he wanted from her, or was he after a deeper relationship? Was he capable of giving her more? She certainly deserved more. Even a blind man could see her caring nature. You only had to see how she was with Davey and her mother, as well as her friends. Brooke wanted to believe people could change. She'd certainly thought Duncan had, and this afternoon he'd seen how she'd looked at her sister. He hoped for Brooke's sake that she and Candice could make things work.

Then there was the fact that Brooke had helped him face the demons of Garry's death. While the guilt still lingered, now he was able to look at it as the tragic accident it was.

For the first time in his life, Mac didn't understand his feelings for a woman. The emotions he felt for Brooke ran far deeper than anything he'd ever experienced before.

He reached over and rested his forearms on the handlebars. It was like Brooke had taken over his soul. He sat back and put his helmet on.

I'll think about this later. First we have to get through setting up the new company.

But maybe he should court her properly ...

***

Brooke sat in the sunroom with Davey, eating her breakfast, when Mathew walked in carrying the morning paper, his usual bright smile replaced with a frown.

"What's wrong?" she asked, knowing she was not going to like whatever it was in the paper.

"It's not good, Miss Brooke."

Fairfax Family Rocked by another Scandal.

The Fairfax family of Bindarra Creek have been rocked by yet another scandal. Gordon Fairfax, Business Manager of Ingalls Development, was charged yesterday with embezzling funds from the family business. It is not known how long Mr Fairfax had been embezzling from the firm his father-in-law, Henry Ingalls, established in 1962. The original office was set up in Bindarra Creek before another office was established in Tamworth.

It is believed that Mr Fairfax had aspirations of running for council in the next election after the retirement of Councilman Roy Towns.

Tuesday of this week, Duncan Fairfax was arrested on charges of arson in relation to the fire-bombing of his sister, Brooke's art studio on her property in Tamworth.

Last week, Brooke Fairfax was caught in a scuffle with another patron at a local Tamworth nightclub.

"Just bloody great," Brooke huffed.

Her mother hurried into the room and sat down. "I'm sorry to say, Brooke, but it gets worse. The front gate is swamped with news crews. We're in for a rough ride."

Mathew walked in carrying a large white box. "This just arrived for you, Miss Brooke."

Brooke lifted the lid and gasped. Nestled in white tissue were a dozen long-stem red roses. The fragrance tickled her nose. An embossed white card lay on top which simply read,

I'm sorry. M.

Her heart pounded in her chest. She ran her fingers over one of the soft petals and smiled.

By the time Brooke made it through the media scrum with the promise a statement would be released later that day, she was running late for her meeting with Mac.

She was determined to show him they had what was needed to make a relationship work. She was in a new mindset. *Take it slow.* She released the breath she didn't know she was holding.

Mac stood there waiting. He pushed a stone around with the toe of his shoe like a nervous kid. She strolled up and placed a kiss on his cheek.

"How are you this morning?" she asked, gazing up into his eyes.

He smiled down at her like an uncle indulging a niece. *This isn't how he's supposed to look at me.* Okay, maybe she should have just kissed him on the lips and been done with it. "Ahh … thank you for my flowers. They're beautiful.

He brushed a finger on the tip of her nose. "You're welcome. Are you ready to get this all sorted?"

Yep, he's in uncle mood. Crap. "Yeah," she answered vaguely.

What the hell was going on? Maybe she should have worn a more revealing outfit. She'd wanted to look professional, so she had opted for a navy suit and a nice pair of black stilettos. The fact that they gave her a bit more height was also a plus. Mac took hold of her elbow as they entered Clarence's office.

Seated at the desk was a pretty blonde, her hair pulled back into a high ponytail. Her face glowed as she looked up at Brooke and Mac.

"Alison, what are you doing here? How lovely to see you," Brooke said excitedly. The last she had heard of Alison Moore was that she had moved to Melbourne.

"Brooke! When Clarence said you were coming in this morning, I near screamed the house down."

"What house?" Brooke asked.

"Clarence and I got married about eight months ago."

Brooke introduced Mac to Alison then spent the next ten minutes catching up with Alison's news since they had last seen each other.

The door opened and Ross walked in, smiling at them all. "Good morning," he greeted.

Clarence came out of his office. "I see you are keeping the clients entertained again, Alison."

Brooke was surprised to see Clarence kiss the top of Alison's head. Clarence always seemed so reserved to Brooke, but it was plain to see these two people were in love.

"It looks like we might be ready to go. Alison, could you order some coffee please?" He shared a secret smile with his wife.

"Sure, honey." She kissed his cheek. "Now, what would you all like?"

The men all ordered straight black coffee. Brooke asked for a soy latte. Alison's face beamed. "Oh good, someone who has good taste at last. I'll just pop over to the Cyprus Café."

Clarence ushered them into his office. "I love her dearly, but she makes a terrible cup of coffee," he said, closing the door behind him.

"I heard that," Alison called through the closed door.

As she took one of the seats facing Clarence's desk, Brooke said. "I'm so happy for you and Ally."

"Thank you, Brooke. That means a lot to both Alison and I. Now, we are here on business. So first off, let's hear what you two have in mind for this venture," Clarence said. "How do you want it to work?"

Brooke glanced over at Mac, not sure what to say.

"To tell you the truth, Clarence, I hadn't thought about it. As you know, I'm new at all this so I guess I'll need to take my lead from you guys." Now she felt like a prize dill. They'd all be thinking she was such an airhead.

"Have you found out how far Fairfax had gone into setting up the subdivision?" Mac asked.

"The proposal is in with council. The word I have is that if it meets all the government regulations, council will have no problem approving the development. Donaldson wants this town back on the map so he'll be pushing for a quick outcome," Clarence said.

"Great. Let's find somewhere in town here for an office to make things easier for Brooke and I," Mac replied.

"Mac, you don't have to do that," she protested. "I'm sure we can come up with something else."

"What? You don't want to be involved in the running of the business?" he asked her. *Great, now I've pissed him off.*

"No, I mean, yes I do. I was just thinking about you having to be here so much." *God, could the ground just open up and swallow me now.*

195

Mac's lips were moving, but Brooke didn't hear a word of what he said. "Sorry, did you say something? Err ... my mind wandered."

"I said I am planning on staying around, so it's no problem."

She couldn't help it, she had to smile. *Yippee, he was staying.* "In that case, we will need to find some office space." She turned to Clarence, smiling brightly. "Do you know of anywhere available, Clarence?"

They'd gone through some possibilities when Alison arrived back with the coffees. "Sorry to be so long, I couldn't get away from Thea and Stavros, you know how they are."

"Thanks, Ally," Clarence said. "Could you ring Hunter Sullivan and see if the shop next to the Cyprus is still for let, please?"

"That would work perfectly if we could have that space." Brooke smiled with excitement.

"You'll need to come up with a company name and get it registered. Plus you'll need an ABN. Your accountant can see to that, or Clarence or I can do it," Ross said.

"Brooke, do you have any ideas?" Mac asked.

She tapped a fingernail against her teeth. "What about Bindarra Horizon Estate? The development is on the east side of town, so that would work in Horizon, and I'd like to have Bindarra in the name to help promote the town."

"Great, that was easy. Ross, could you register that with ASIC for us?" Mac asked.

"I can ask Raymond Brothers to do the ABN for us," Brooke said, getting into the swing of things. She already had ideas for a logo and artwork for signs; she had to stop herself from hugging Mac, thus blowing her new professional image out of the water.

This adventure was going to work.

At the end of the meeting, Brooke took Clarence to one side and asked if he could release a statement to the media about her father's arrest.

***

Later that afternoon, Mac met up with Brooke out the front of the real estate agency owned by Hunter Sullivan. Sullivan was dressed in bone moleskin jeans and a blue chambray shirt bearing the logo of his business. The guy looked the part of a country real estate agent. Over his brown hair, he wore an Akubra hat. "Hunter, this is Mac Stafford. Mac, Hunter Sullivan," Brooke introduced the men.

After shaking hands, Hunter turned his attention to Brooke. Mac had seen the guy when they both had been running of a morning. Although they had never spoken, they often waved to each other.

Mac's body reacted in the most primal way when Brooke bit her lower lip. *Damn, I don't know if I'll survive working with her. I wonder if there is a shower in the building. If not, I'll have one put in.*

Hunter handed Mac the keys. "Take your time looking over the building. If I can help in any way, just let me know."

Mac opened the door. The room had the

overpowering smell of rodent droppings, mould and damp paper. Leaving the door open, they walked around the area. It was in a prime location for the Horizon office with plenty of parking at the rear of the building.

Mac was impressed with the size of the area. They would be able to have separate offices for both him and Brooke. She plagued his dreams every night, he didn't need her invading his concentration all day.

A small reception area could be set up in the front of the building, which would mean they'd need to hire a receptionist. There were enough unemployed young people in town that it wouldn't be hard to find someone.

"What do you think, Brooke?" he asked, watching her as she roamed about the room. *Damn she has great legs.* The high heels made her legs look like they went on forever. His body tightened.

She turned and smiled which for the first time in days, reached her eyes. "It's wonderful. We can have two to three offices and a reception area at the front." She used her hands to show where each area could be located. "A couple of lounge chairs for clients. I hate the hard seats some places have. When we have it painted and new carpet laid, it will look fantastic. I know a builder who could do the work for us. Nash Johnson lives across the road from us. He and his father run Bindarra Building Company."

Mac leaned a shoulder against the wall and folded his arms over his chest. He was pleased to see Brooke get carried away with the plans for the office.

"Do you happen to know of a painter, electrician and plumber?"

She walked over and rested her back against the wall beside him. Her perfume reminded him of an exotic flower.

"There are a few people in town I'd like us to use. I think if they show they're competent, we might be able to hire them for the subdivision as well." She turned her head and gazed up at him. "I'm so excited."

"Yeah, me too." He dropped his eyes to her lips. Time to move. *Yep, shower definitely being installed.*

***

After signing the required paperwork with Hunter, Brooke and Mac stood in front of the real estate office staring at each other. This was awkward. Had they gotten to the stage where they no longer knew what to say to each other unless it was related to the land subdivision? Brooke had been so sure Mac would kiss her back there in the shop the way his eyes had dropped to her lips, but then he'd blinked and it was back to business.

"Well, I best—"

"Do you want—?"

"Sorry, you go first," Brooke said.

"I was just wondering if you'd like to get a coffee," he replied.

"Oh, um ... I was going to call in and see Ruth Edwards. I haven't seen her since I've been home." She did the hand wavy thing she did when nervous.

Lord, I'm like a bloody schoolgirl. This is ridiculous. I'm a grown woman, act like one.

"Well, that's okay. Give me a call once you've spoken to Johnson." He put his hands in his pockets and turned away.

No, don't let him go. Think.

"Um, you could come and visit Ruth with me if you'd like, she'll enjoy the company." *Now I sound desperate.*

He glanced over his shoulder. "I'd like that. I didn't get much time to chat with her the other day after I'd given her car a service."

"It seems like you know a lot of the older ladies in town. What about the younger ones?" She arched an eyebrow and prayed she didn't sound jealous.

He gave a laugh that melted her bones. "I know a few of the older ones. I guess they remind me of my grandmothers." His eyes sparkled with humour. "And no, I don't know many of the younger women. The only one I want to know only seems to argue with me."

Brooke cleared her throat. "Right, well do you want to come with me? I don't see your bike."

"I walked up from Fred's."

They turned to her car parked across the road in front of the Doctor's surgery.

"Why haven't you moved out of the flat?" Brooke licked her lips.

Mac shrugged. "I don't see any reason to. I'm still doing some work for Fred, plus I promised Russel I'd teach him about being a mechanic."

Brooke clicked the button on the key remote, unlocking her car. "That's good of you."

"Not really, working with cars helps me relax, so it's no big deal to show Russ while I work."

"When did you have time to get your mechanic's license?"

"I took some time off between high school and uni to get my mechanic's ticket. I work on restoring bikes and cars in my spare time." He shrugged as he climbed in on the passenger side.

"Davey was disappointed he missed you yesterday," she said as she pulled out into the main street.

"I'm sorry. I shouldn't have run off like that. I'd intended to spend time with Davey. He's a great kid."

"Yes, he is. He loves having Tyrelle stay with us. He now has five adults running around after him." She bit her lip. "While we're apologising, I owe you one for what I said yesterday in the study. I didn't mean it, I said it in anger and I hurt you. So I'm sorry."

He was quiet for so long Brooke wondered if he was going to reply.

"I overstepped the line as well. Let's put it behind us, maybe we should just start again with everything."

Did he mean he didn't want to remember the magic between them? Because that's what it was to her—a once in a lifetime connection.

CHAPTER THIRTEEN

Arriving at Ruth Edwards' house, Brooke parked out the front then leaned over into the back seat and picked up the basket of slices Ellen had made.

Mac held open the gate, and they walked up a path lined on both sides with beds of roses in three different colours. The delicate perfume followed them to the veranda. Ruth's roses often won the exhibits at the local show.

The front door was open, but the screen door locked, no doubt to stop anyone from walking inside unannounced. Brooke knocked. The hall was dimly lit, so it was hard to see in the house.

"Ruth, are you there?" Brooke leaned forward, placing her hand on the screen to see if she could see into the house.

A muffled sound came from the back.

Heart pounding, she reached for Mac. "Mac, she sounds hurt."

"I'll go around the back."

"She keeps the side gate locked." Feeling helpless, Brooke rubbed a finger against her temple.

"I'll get through." Mac squeezed her hand and gave her an encouraging smile that did little to dispel her unease. He jumped over the side of the veranda, the gate rattled, and heavy footsteps faded up the side of the house.

"Ruth, Mac is coming around the back. He'll be there soon," Brooke yelled through the screen door.

Then Mac's tall frame was silhouetted in the darkness of the hall.

"Ambulance to sixteen Wattle Drive, Bindarra Creek," Mac said into his phone as he unlocked the screen door for Brooke. He waved her forward. "She's in the kitchen."

Brooke nodded and raced down the polished floorboards to the kitchen at the back of the house.

Ruth was lying on her back, her glasses held limply in her hand, her eyes closed. Dropping the basket on the table, Brooke knelt down beside her friend and picked up her cold hand.

"Ruth, can you hear me?" Brooke's heart felt like it was ready to explode from her chest.

"Yes, dear." Her voice was weak and she did not open her eyes. Ruth's face was pale against the tiled floor.

Lord, she could have broken something. "Do you know what happened? Are you hurt anywhere?"

"No, I'm not sure. I came in from the back garden and then you were calling out to me and I was on the floor."

Mac entered the kitchen carrying a white cashmere blanket and pillow. With gentle care, he placed Ruth's head on the pillow then covered her with the blanket, his posture rigid as if he found it hard to control his emotions.

"They want you to stay on the floor until they get here to check you over, Ruth," he said rubbing the woman's hand. Brooke could see the anguish in his eyes.

"I'll ring Mum. She'll want to know." Brooke stood on shaky legs and sank into a chair nearby. Her finger felt numb as she dialed the house number.

"Mathew, it's Brooke. Could I speak to Mum, please?"

Brooke ran a shaky hand across her forehead, feeling terribly helpless.

"Mum?"

"Where are you, dear?"

"Mum, I'm at Ruth's. She's had an accident." Her mother gasped. "Mac's called the ambulance."

"I'll ... I'll be there shortly."

"There's no need for that, Mum, I'll go—"

"I said I'll be there," her mother said brusquely.

Brooke frowned, surprised by her mother's reaction.

The whir of the siren ended as the ambulance pulled up in front of the house. Brooke hurried forward, opening the door. Chat Newland raced up the path while Monty Langer removed the stretcher from the back of the ambulance.

"How long has she been down, Brooke?"

Brooke worried her bottom lip. "I'm not sure. She was on the floor when Mac and I got here ten minutes ago."

They found Mac kneeling beside Ruth, talking to her in a soft reassuring tone.

Mac patted her hand. "Here they are now." He stood up and moved out of the way for Chat to administer the aid needed.

Brooke took a seat and reached for the hand Mac placed on her shoulder.

Chat asked Ruth some questions as he took her blood pressure and when Monty arrived with the stretcher he knelt down on the other side of Ruth.

Her mother arrived not long after, her eyes wide and her hand covering her chest. "How is she? What do you know?" she asked hurriedly.

Brooke stood and eased her mother onto the seat. "Nothing yet, Mum."

Chat continued to speak to Ruth in lowered tones, making it hard to hear. Standing he turned to them, Mac rested a hand on Brooke's back, calming her as Chat spoke.

"Mrs Edwards hasn't any broken bones and her heart rate is strong, but her blood pressure is a bit low. Monty and I'll transport her up to the Polyclinic for the doctor to have a look at her."

"Wi ... will she need to go into Armidale?" Louise stammered.

"I shouldn't think so, Mrs Fairfax, but that will be up to Doctor Hill once she's had a chance to examine Mrs Edwards."

Her mother turned and held Brooke's hand. It felt like ice. "I'll go to the Polyclinic with Ruth, dear. Could you gather some items she'll need for a prolonged stay with us?"

Brooke drew her brows together. Her mother was acting very peculiar. "Of course, I'll have a room made up for Ruth as soon as I get home." She kissed her mother's cheek.

"If you give me your keys, Louise, I'll follow in your car and then I can drive you and Ruth home."

Louise turned to Mac, a faint smile on her lips. "I would appreciate that, Mac." She turned to Brooke, her brows furrowed. "Please ask Ellen to prepare your Grandpa's suite for m ... Ruth, dear?"

"Of course." No one had used her grandpa's suite since his death. Brooke wondered again, what was going on between her mother and Ruth.

Mac stood beside Brooke as Chat and Monty secured Ruth to the stretcher. He gave her hand a gentle squeeze. "I'll see you back at the house."

She nodded then rushed off to gather the items Ruth would need to make herself comfortable for her stay.

***

Mac drove up with Louise and Ruth seated in the back of the car. Lights illuminated the front of the house. Brooke stood on the step wringing her hands. He strode around the front of the car, opened the back passenger door and lifted Ruth into his arms.

"Mac, I can walk," Ruth said with a blush on her cheeks.

Mac laughed. "I'll carry you. I'm sure Louise wouldn't want to take any chances on you fainting again."

Brooke opened the door and stood to one side as they entered, knowing he would stay for as long as he was needed.

"Go through, grandpa's room is at the back of the house," Brooke directed. "Davey's in his room with Tyrelle. She's reading him a story."

Her mother reached for her hand. "Thank you, dear. I feel dreadful for missing dinner with him."

Mac made his way to the rooms followed closely by Louise and Brooke. The suite consisted of a small sitting room that led into a spacious bedroom and an ensuite to one side.

He lowered Ruth to the bed and stepped back. "I'll wait outside in case you need me again."

"Thank you, Mac. Could you ask Ellen to bring in some tea for us, please?" said Louise.

"Of course."

Mac walked into the kitchen to find Ellen and Mathew chatting with an elderly woman. Without the hustle and bustle of his previous visit, the room had a welcoming vibe. It was a room where meals were cooked with love.

"Louise asked if you could prepare a tray of tea please, Ellen."

"I've heard about you, sonny," the woman said.

Her long grey hair was pulled back in a loose bun, with a long strand plaited with beads and feathers hanging down the side of her face. Mac tried to hide his amusement, but obviously failed.

"My granddaughter Kaylee did my hair. I think she did quite a good job of it."

"It's very becoming."

She ran her eyes over him as if trying to assess if he was friend or foe. He stared, not breaking eye contact. A smile broke out across her face.

"I'm Edwina Lette. That's Ms not Mrs" She held her hand out.

Mac took the slim aged hand. "It's a pleasure to meet you, Ms Lette."

She glanced up with a worried frown. "You have some major hurdles to conquer before you find happiness."

Mac blinked, not sure how to reply. Brooke entered the room saving him from any further discussion.

"Mac, Mum asked if you could assist with helping Ruth to the recliner in the sitting room."

"I'll be happy to. Lovely to meet you, Ms Lette." He left the room with a chill sitting between his shoulder blades.

***

"Ms Lette, as always it's lovely to see you," Brooke said. "I love your new hair style."

Brooke had always liked Dodge Myers' grandmother. She was one of the most colourful members of the town.

"The pleasure is mine, Brooke." Ms Lette gave her an odd look. "Give me your hand, child."

Knowing what was coming, Brooke opened her hand to the older woman curiously.

"Love is on your door, but take care." Ms Lette dropped her hand. "Now, take me to see Ruth. I've been worried since I heard of her fall."

Brooke and Ms Lette entered the sitting room to find Ruth propped up in a reclining chair with a cashmere rug over her legs.

"Edwina, what are you doing here?" Ruth held her hand out.

The women clasped hands as if they were a lifeline for each other.

"I heard what had happened and had to see you were all right. Tessa dropped me off." Ms Lette glanced around the room. "Tessa is Dodge's young lady. I couldn't be happier if she were my own granddaughter. Her daughter Kaylee is a treasure, makes me feel young again."

Ruth gave an unladylike snort. "You? Feel old? That will be the day!"

Brooke pressed her lips together and tried not to

laugh.

Ms Lette took a seat next to Ruth on one of the sofas and waved her hand. "Yes, yes, enough about me. What of you?"

"I'll let Louise explain. She was able to take in more than me."

Mathew entered with a tray holding an assortment of cakes with cups, a teapot and coffee pot. He left without a word and closed the door behind him. After asking what everyone wanted and distributing the tea and coffee, Brooke took a seat on the other sofa.

"Take a seat, Mac. This may take some time," Louise said and sat next to Ms Lette.

The only spot left was next to Brooke. As his thigh touched hers, it sent heat surging through her body. Ms Lette gave them a knowing look.

"Doctor Hill said Ruth had a blackout called syncope, it is caused by a problem in the regulation of blood pressure, sometimes with the heart," her mother said.

Brooke gasped.

"Karen checked Ruth over and her heart is good, although her blood pressure was low. It's not a major problem, but it is best that Ruth isn't left by herself in case it happens again. So Ruth will be moving in here with us and can decide what she would like to do with her house sometime in the future," her mother finished.

Silence fell over the room for a moment before Ms

Lette looked at Louise and said, "I take it you know who Ruth is?"

"Yes." She nodded.

"Maybe this is where I should leave," Mac said, placing his cup on the table.

"No, stay. I think you've worked it out," her mother replied.

Brooke glanced around the room as Mac's strong fingers closed around her hand. Was there a big secret everyone was keeping from her? *This can't be good.*

Louise glanced at Ruth. "Would you like to tell the story or shall I?"

Ruth gazed into her teacup. "You go ahead, dear. I'm sure Edwina will be able to fill in any blank spots."

The women clasped hands again and smiled encouragingly at each other.

After all this time, they still had such a strong friendship, Brooke thought.

Ruth and Ms Lette were chalk and cheese. Ruth always dressed conservatively with not a hair out of place and had a soft well-mannered voice, while Ms Lette wore free-flowing skirts and loose tops, normally with gumboots like she had on today.

Ms Lette had a tendency to say whatever popped into her head, and occasionally smoked her 'medicinal' rollies. It would not have surprised Brooke if Edwina Lette was Bindarra Creek's original wild child.

"Before Dad passed away he told me a few things he felt I needed to know." Louise licked her lips. "I'd guessed most of the story when I was younger, but waited for Dad's confirmation."

Brooke glanced at her mother and Ruth. *Lord, Mum looks as nervous as Ruth.*

Louise explained how Ruth was in fact Brooke's grandmother, and why Brooke's grandpa Henry and Ruth never married.

Ms Lette took up the telling of the story. "Henry was engaged to Nanny Higgins, but she called the wedding off three months before the event. Nancy had become infatuated with a travelling salesman. In that time, Henry started dating Ruth, everyone with half an eye could see they were in love. The fancy salesman left town without the besotted Miss Higgins." Ms Lette drew in a breath and shook her head. "Well, Nancy was pea green with envy when she saw Henry and Ruth about town happy as any lovebirds could be. The next thing you know Nancy announces she's pregnant and that Henry would have to marry her after all.

Well, Henry being the kind of man he was, did the right thing and married Nancy. This bit was not known around town, but Nancy had a miscarriage around the time that Ruth discovered she was with child. Not wanting her child to grow up not knowing either of its parents, Ruth gave Louise up to Henry and Nancy."

It was a sad story and one that broke Brooke's

heart.

"I always knew there was a connection between us," Brooke whispered as she went and knelt by her grandmother's chair.

Ruth gave her an encouraging smile, but her cheeks were pale.

"I think it's time we left so Ruth can get some rest. It's been a big day and we don't want to overtax her." Brooke looked at Mac, allowing him to see her concern. "Would you mind helping Ruth to bed so she can have a lie down please?"

"I can walk, dear," Ruth protested.

"No, I'll carry you. You wouldn't want me to get into trouble with that headstrong granddaughter of yours, would you?"

Damn, why does he always have to be so nice to elderly women and kids?

***

Mac followed the women into the sitting room. Brooke's back was as straight as a rod, her steps almost jerky. She'd had a lot to take in the last hour. It couldn't be easy finding out the grandmother you'd known wasn't really your grandparent. It had been plain to see the closeness she shared with Ruth, and this was sure to grow now Brooke knew of their relationship.

"Would you like a cup of tea, Edwina?" Louise asked.

"That would be nice, and then I'll ring Tessa and ask her to pick me up."

Brooke turned to Mac, her face an unreadable mask. "If you take my car, Mac, you could drop Ms Lette home."

"Sure, but do you trust me with your car? I might just take off and never return." He smiled.

Her eyes lit up with a hint of mischief. "I think I can trust you."

The simple statement hit him in the solar plexus. Mac ran his hands through his hair. *Do I deserve Brooke's trust? What if I let her down? Damn, it's just a bloody car, not her life.*

Edwina Lette crowed with laughter. "Well, won't that get up Pamela Brown's nose, seeing me arrive home in that fancy car of yours, Brooke, and driven by such a handsome young man!"

Brooke and Louise saw Mac and his lively passenger out to the car half an hour later. The sun was setting, giving the sky a soft orange glow. Mac loved to watch the sunset. It always had a calming effect on him.

"Juzz Mac," Davey's excited shriek came from inside the house, followed by the sound of little feet running on the marble floor.

Mac crouched down, waiting. It didn't take long for the fair-haired boy to burst through the doorway and down the steps.

Davey wrapped his arms around Mac's neck. It surprised Mac how attached he'd become to the little boy.

"Juzz Mac, play with Davey."

Mac stood, taking the boy in his arms up with him. "I have to go home now, buddy, but I'll be back tomorrow. Can we play then?"

Davey's eyes filled with tears.

I should have made time for Davey rather than having another cup of coffee. Mac ruffled Davey's hair. "Tell you what, I'll come over for breakfast then we can play for a bit before Brooke and I have to do some work, okay?"

"Kay." The wide smile he received touched his heart.

Mac put Davey down and watched as the boy ran to Brooke, wrapping his arms around her legs. *Don't think of those legs.*

"I'll make a list of the things we'll need to get started on tomorrow, Mac," Brooke's husky voice carried to him.

God, save me from women with lists.

CHAPTER FOURTEEN

The next morning Davey rose in a mood of over-the-top excitement. In between mouthfuls of cereal, he'd run off to check whether Mac had arrived or not. Brooke found the action quite sweet, and now and then she joined Davey in the search. Of course, it had nothing to do with the fact that she was excited to see Mac as well. No, theirs was a business arrangement, that's all. Full stop. The end.

When Davey heard Brooke's car come to a stop in the drive, he let out a squeal through his cupped hands. "Juzz Mac here, Roo and Elle, Juzz Mac here."

Brooke hurried after him concerned Davey might jump and fall if Mac wasn't ready to catch him. She needn't have worried. Mac was waiting to catch him as he jumped from the steps into Mac's arms.

"Juzz Mac, you come to play with Davey."

"That I did, little buddy." Mac glanced at Davey then at Brooke in the doorway.

Her heart hit the bottom of her stomach before it settled back in her chest. *Lordy, Lordy, and I have to spend all day with him.*

"Good morning, Mac." She forced a bright smile on her lips. He was dressed once again in his dark suit that made him look all business.

"Good morning to you too, princess."

It's going to be a long day.

Tyrelle sat cross-legged on the floor, setting up the Hungry Hippo game when they walked into the sitting room.

"We play Hungry Hippo, Juzz Mac."

Mac removed his jacket and sat cross-legged on the floor next to Davey with no concern for his suit pants. "I've never played this game before so you'll have to tell me how to play."

Davey gave Mac a sombre look before explaining the rules while Brooke sat in front of her hippo mouth and watched the interplay between man and boy. Mac listened intently to each of Davey's explanations, nodding to acknowledge his understanding.

Soon Davey was happy that Mac understood the rules clapped his hands and said, "Let's play."

The three adults sat around the game with Davey, everyone frantically trying to get as many balls as possible. They'd spent an hour playing when Mathew came in telling them it was time for breakfast.

Her mother and Ruth joined them in the kitchen, where a round table with six chairs stood by a window overlooking the back garden. It was a noisy meal with Davey entertaining them all. Brooke stole glances at Mac, only to find him watching her too.

At nine o'clock, Brooke and Mac rose saying it was time for them to get to work. Brooke led the way into the office which had undertaken a remodelling in the past week, making it lighter and more welcoming. White shutters replaced the once heavy drapes, the walls papered with a Chinese scene in cream and white. Where there were once photos of her father covering the walls, now photos of family took pride of place.

Mac whistled through his teeth. "You and Louise have been working hard."

She glanced around the room with a broad smile. "Not really. We had a woman from Tamworth come in and do the work for us. Angela has worked wonders in such a short space of time. The painters were in on Thursday afternoon and then she had a troop of workers in here yesterday putting up the wallpaper, shutters and doing the final changes. We're happy with the result."

"Have you heard anything about your father and brother?" Mac asked, sitting down on one of the sofas that overlooked the drive.

Brooke pulled a notepad from the desk and took the other seat, placing the pad and a pen on the low table.

"Both Father and Duncan's cases go to court in December. I'll be glad when it's all over and done with, then Mum can concentrate on the work needed for Ingalls. We've talked about bringing Candice back into the business, but we'll wait and see." She picked up the pad with nervous hands and handed it to Mac. "I've a list of things I think we need to do if you'd like to look at it and see if I've missed anything."

Brooke wrung her hands while she waited for Mac to speak. Mathew arrived with the coffee and left without a word while Mac continued to go over the list. Brooke stood and walked about the room picking up little objects for something to do so she wouldn't look over Mac's shoulder to explain things.

It's not that long a bloody list. Why is he taking so long?

"This all looks good to me. If we think of anything else as we go along we can add to it, but you have made a good start."

Brooke released the breath she held. "Good, and then I think it would be best if we go to the bank and open the account for Horizon. Raymond has sent me through the information we'll need."

Mac accepted the cup of coffee she handed to him then reached for a ginger biscuit.

"I know a few people we can use for the subdivision. They're all local so it will keep the work in Bindarra Creek. As I said yesterday, there's Nash Johnson across the road."

Brooke's gaze followed as Mac lifted the cup to his lips. *What I wouldn't give for that to be my lips.* She gave herself a mental shake. *We're here to work. Not to have silly romantic thoughts or dreams.* Although dreams were a lot harder to control, and she'd had many a dream these past few nights.

"If you're happy to ring around and see if you can set up a meeting at some point, I'd like to work for Fred this afternoon. There are a couple of jobs that need doing. One is a leftover from yesterday. Also, I've organised for Russ to come in this afternoon."

"He must be excited."

"I think he is. I'm sure he'll make a good mechanic."

Brooke stood without touching her coffee. "I guess we should be on our way."

She didn't wait to see if Mac followed. A tight frown formed on her brow. *So we won't be spending all day together. That's good, I'm happy about that.* So why did she feel like she'd lost her favourite teddy? *Stupid is what it is.*

Once they had the account sorted to her and Mac's satisfaction, they left the bank to look at the office space again.

"I'd like to get Greg Atkinson in to give the office a good paint, as well as tidy up the front, and I know a guy in Tamworth who could do the signage for us off my artwork. I'll also contact Nash about building the offices and the reception area. What do you think?"

"Sounds good. You're on top of this, it seems. If

you can chase them up tomorrow, we can sit down and work out any other issues that need exploring. If you have enough to keep you busy today, I'll get going to Fred's."

What am I the little run-around girl? "Sure, not a problem." *Well, he can bloody walk to Fred's in his damn suit and all.*

***

Mac headed back to the garage, stopping to talk to people along the way. In the end, a walk that should have taken him fifteen minutes took forty-five.

He had a quick shower before pulling on his jeans and T-shirt. He didn't think he'd ever be able to go back to working in an office full-time again. And he sure as hell would not live in Sydney again. Bindarra Creek was more like his home now. He loved the relaxed life.

Russel was waiting for him when he returned. It didn't take long for Mac to realise that Russel had a knack for this sort of work.

No, I can't leave until I finish training Russel, which would take a very long time. Time enough to court Brooke.

Thinking of which he made a phone call.

***

Brooke spent the afternoon closeted in the home office making calls to the people they needed on their team. She started with Mark Bradford, who had done some work for Rupert at his art gallery, asking if he would be interested in designing six houses for a display village then told him he was welcome to use space in the Horizon office so he could work out of Bindarra Creek. He seemed happy with that as he had also taken on some restoration work with the grant the town had secured a few months back.

Mark Bradford—check.

Next she rang Nash Johnson. He agreed to work on the office space for Horizon as well as build the display houses.

Nash Johnson—check

Trent Green, plumber—check

Greg Atkinson, painter—check

Jolene Lawrence, electrician—check

Ring Clarence re-proposal—check

Ring surveyor—check

Just as she was ready to stop for the day, Mathew walked in with a large flower arrangement of red roses and baby's breath in a crystal vase. A simple hand-written card was tucked onto a white cardholder.

See you tomorrow. M

The air rushed from her lungs. She was sure if anyone walked in and saw her, she'd have a silly smile on her face. Thank heavens she had her back to Mathew.

***

Mac pulled up in front of Brooke's home a little after nine the next morning. Mathew told him Davey was already off on some adventure with Tyrelle, and that Brooke was in the office. He walked in to find

Brooke seated behind the overly large timber desk, paper scattered everywhere. His flowers sat on the corner of the desk.

"What's this all about" He smiled lazily and lifted up a sheet of figures.

"I know we still have to wait for the right figures to come in, but I thought if we had an idea of what we could make on the subdivision it might help."

Mac frowned. "Brooke, we can't work a business this way. We need set numbers. Our accountant will work these out. I can have Paul up here tomorrow."

"No, the idea of this is to use local trade. We are trying to build up the town, not bring in outside help unless there's no one here to do the job. Raymond is more than suitable, he handles all Ingalls accounts."

Mac prowled the office, running his hands through his hair.

"Why don't you sit," Brooke offered, but he ignored her.

"Tell me what you did yesterday."

"I organised appointments with most of the trades. I spent some time going over figures and percentages that we can use for selling each block of land." She handed him a spreadsheet. "Now this is an approximate costing for each house. I was thinking if we could sell each house with us receiving ten percent to cover overheads—"

"Ten percent! Are you crazy, woman? We'd be broke within the year. Brooke, businesses need to make a decent profit to stay viable. Why don't you stick with the everyday running of the office and let me deal with the important side of it, that way we'll all come out winners."

He looked up to see Brooke's eyes ablaze with anger, her body stiff and her slim hands fisted.

Mac ran a hand through his hair. *Shit, I'm in for it now.*

"So I do the mundane things, do I?" she spat at him, her hands on hips. "What, I don't have a business brain in my head?"

"Yes, no, it's just that we all have our talents. Yours is your art."

Shit, she's going to cry. Mac sighed with relief when not a single tear dropped.

"Get out. Get out now before I do something quite physically harmful to you."

"Princess—"

"Don't go bloody 'princessing' me, you overstated baboon. Now get out," she shouted. Picking up the vase with the roses in it, she shoved them into his hands. "And take your bloody flowers with you."

He stood outside the office, shoulders slumped. *Why couldn't I just keep my bloody mouth shut and talk to her calmly? Maybe I should ring my dad.*

No, he knew what he had done wrong. He had belittled her idea. Hell, they could afford to run the business to only break even. As long as they didn't lose money, they'd be fine. *I'd better send a larger bouquet of roses with an apology note.*

He walked into the foyer as Louise was coming

down the stairs. She glanced at the flowers then up to his face. Obviously, his expression said it all.

"How many roses are you sending this time?"

"Five dozen." he said running a hand through his hair.

"That bad?" Louise arched an eyebrow and gave him a knowing smile, then took the flowers from his arms. "I think a personal apology would be best. That is if you want to apologise."

***

Curled up in the corner of the sofa, Brooke reached for a tissue and wiped the tears from her cheeks then reached for another tissue and blew her nose. Her eyes felt like the size of golf balls, and her nose was no doubt as red as a clown's.

Good thing no one can see me.

She rubbed at the heaviness in her chest as another ripping sob escaped through her trembling lip. The saltiness of her tears hung on her tongue as she licked her lips. She threw the used tissues on the floor and pulled out more to repeat the process again.

The door to the office opened slowly. "Princess?"

"G ... go ... a ... way." Another sob wracked her aching body.

Mac stepped into the room, his hair dishevelled, his tie hung loosely from his collar and his top button was undone. He walked over and picked her up from the sofa before sitting down with her on his lap.

"I don ... don't ... want ... y ... you he ... here," she sobbed into his chest.

"I know, princess." He kissed the top of her head. "I'm sorry. I'm such an arse."

"I kn ... know."

"I should have listened to you. Your idea is a good one." He kissed her brow.

She lifted her head. "Really?"

"Yes." He kissed her eyes.

Brooke pulled back. "You're not just saying that?"

"No. It's a great idea, a brilliant way to draw people to the area." His gaze was intent and honest. He leaned forward, kissed her cheek and pulled a handful of tissues from the box to wipe her face. Holding one at her nose, he said, "Blow."

She did and then he sank back into the sofa and held her on his lap, lightly running his fingers up her arm. Brooke snuggled down her head against his chest and closed her eyes with a sigh.

***

On Monday morning Brooke and Mac decided to play hooky to spend time with Davey and to give Tyrelle time to go home and pick up some more clothes. She'd encouraged her friend to hand in her notice to the landlord. Everyone loved having Tyrelle around, and she had no real reason to turn to Tamworth.

Mac suggested they go out to the Akuna National Park and do one of the small trail walks. Davey ran along in front of them, looking for interesting rocks and leaves, and placing them in his Buzz Lightyear backpack. A slight breeze rustled the leaves, native birds called mating chirps to one another. It was a beautiful Spring day, and Brooke was as content as she'd ever been. And in love.

***

Around lunchtime on Tuesday, Brooke was driving back from Tamworth after visiting Mark Bradford, drumming her fingers on the steering wheel in time to Metallica blaring through the speakers. She spared a quick glance at Fred's where Mac had started back working afternoons. They'd spent this morning going over her final artwork for the posters and office front. Mac now spent his nights at her place, which Davey loved as he had breakfast and dinner with his hero. She smiled, looking forward to that night when they would lie in each other's arms.

Everything in her world was perfect.

She was happy with what she had achieved that day. With the stationary sorted and Mark locked in to come on board, all was going to plan. Brooke had been impressed with Mark's designs. They showed fresh, innovative ideas along with conventional styles. She had a good feeling about the day.

A red four-wheel drive travelling east along the road swerved to Brooke's side of the road. She turned the steering wheel to avoid a head-on collision, but her car was slammed sideways, jarring her body. The airbags inflated. Her body catapulted forward then backward, her head hitting hard against the headrest. Pain gripped her side. She felt helpless as the impact of the collision rotated her car like a child's spinning top. She thought it would never stop. Her focus came in and out. The world looked like a sea of disjointed colours. Agony splintered through her body. A scream rang through her ears before she realized it was she who was screaming then darkness descended, closing off her pain.

CHAPTER FIFTEEN

Mac ran from the back of the garage workshop at the first sound of metal-on-metal, the ear-piercing screech of car brakes and horns. The crashing thud of metal and glass hitting the road echoed in the late afternoon silence. Beth and Fred emerged from the café as he took off running down the street.

As he drew closer, his lungs threatened to collapse inside his chest. *No, no, oh God no!* Mac had never believed that one's heart could stop for a moment in time, but his did. The sight of Brooke's car a twisted wreck of metal met his horrified gaze.

"I've called for emergency services," Cameron Reid said as he ran toward Mac from the farm supply store.

Mac nodded. He heaved air into his lungs as he

dropped beside the driver's window. The door crushed into Brooke's seat.

"Brooke, princess, can you hear me?" He almost wept. Crimson blood seeped from a cut on her head, a stark contrast to the pale complexion of her skin.

Her chest rose and fell with the rhythm of her breathing. Mac stood and checked over the car for any sign of flames or fuel leaks.

"She's safe, Mac," Cameron assured him.

"Tha ... thanks." This couldn't be happening. It was a nightmare.

"I didn't see her, I swear, I didn't see her until it was too late," came the wobbly voice beside Mac. "The sun was in my eyes. I was reaching for my sunnies."

Mac turned and glared at the teenager standing behind him. He looked no older than Russel. Mac swallowed the harsh reply he was set to serve the youngster. He'd have enough guilt without Mac adding to it.

"Come on, mate," Cameron said, leading the boy away, talking calmly.

Sirens blared from the centre of town. *Thank God, they'll be here soon.*

He knelt back down by the window. "They're coming, princess. Hang on."

Raised voices fell over the gathering crowd. Mac stepped back as firefighters and paramedics rushed to Brooke's aid. Kel Jones, one of the fieries, carried the jaws-of-life to crank open the door. Chat told him to step back so he could place a neck brace on Brooke to help protect her from any further injuries.

Riley Hunter, the local Senior Sergeant, had arrived and was talking to the teenager. The kid looked ready to pass out.

It all swirled around Mac like it was happening in someone else's life—not his, not Brooke's, not their lives.

Soft arms wrapped around his waist. "She'll be fine, Mac," Beth said.

Mac cleared his throat. "Can you and Fred go out and tell Louise? I don't want her hearing this news on the phone."

"I have the ute here all ready to go, son," Fred replied, scratching his head. "I've locked up the garage. Beth, we best be off. We'll bring Louise to the hospital."

"Thanks," Mac said absently as he watched Brooke finally lifted out onto the trauma board then transferred to the stretcher. His heart pounded so hard he could feel it against his chest. He ran over to the ambulance.

An oxygen mask covered her nose and lips. She looked deathly white.

"Is she okay?"

Chat turned and met his frantic gaze. "She hasn't regained consciousness yet. Her blood pressure is down some. We'll give her oxygen on the way."

"Chat, I'm coming with you. Fred and Beth have gone to get Louise." He'd be damned if he would let anyone try to stop him.

"Mac." Chat shook his head then said, "Very well, but you'll have to sit in the front."

Mac would have argued, but knew he'd pushed as far as he could so he nodded his agreement. He jumped into the passenger seat and waited for Monty Langer to join him.

The trip to Armidale seemed to take forever, his hands became sweaty, his heart raced, and his body shook.

"It won't be long, mate," Monty said beside him.

Mac closed his eyes, wanting to squelch the nightmare that had unfolded before his eyes. *I can't lose her. Not after Garry, not now, not when I finally found someone I love as deeply as Brooke.*

Monty drove into the ambulance waiting bay at Armidale Hospital. Mac jumped out as soon as it stopped and raced to the back. He had to wait long minutes before they unloaded Brooke from the back of the ambulance.

"Has she ..." He couldn't finish the sentence, but knew from the look in Chat's eyes that she hadn't yet opened her beautiful jade eyes. He held her hand as she was ferried into the Emergency Room. Nurses came from all directions to assist.

"You'll have to leave while we examine your wife, sir," said a nurse dressed in blue scrubs.

"Not my wife," Mac replied, watching as Brooke was lifted from the stretcher to the bed. "Not yet."

"I'll send someone to talk to you soon." She pushed

him towards the door leading to what Mac guessed was the waiting room. He wanted to fight, tell them he couldn't leave her side, and tell them she was the only person that made him feel whole, but he didn't. *I'll tell that to Brooke and only Brooke.*

The smell of disinfectant, blood and body sweat hung in the air. Groans and patients calling to nurses rang out from behind the closed doors. As he paced back and forth over the length of the waiting room he ran his hands through his hair.

I shouldn't have left. She needs me. I need her.

An elderly woman came towards him. She gave him a kind smile. "I'm Sarah Lovett, a social worker here. I believe you're a friend of Ms Fairfax's," she said quietly.

She went into what Mac guessed was the normal story they gave people not related to a patient. They were doing tests, Brooke was doing okay under the circumstances.

"Thank you," his voice sounded disembodied. *This can't be happening.*

The woman left him to his misery.

She'll be fine, she has to be. I won't lose another person I love.

He returned to his pacing. The curious eyes of other visitors watched him, but he paid no heed to them. When the door to the waiting room opened, Louise entered, her face pale and eyes red and swollen. Beth and Fred followed close on her heels.

"How is she? Have you heard anything?" Louise

reached out to clasp his hands. Hers felt as cold as his. "Where is she?"

"She hasn't woken up yet. They won't let me in to see her because I'm not family," he bit out. *She needs me, I know she does.*

"I'll see to it," Louise whispered, racing over to the triage nurse's window.

Fred and Beth came to his side, but said nothing. Beth held his hand, squeezing his fingers periodically.

Moments later, Louise returned. "We'll be able to go in shortly before they move her to the intensive care unit."

The door to the emergency opened. A tall, slim nurse stood in the doorway. "Mrs Fairfax?"

Beth let go of his hand, as Louise stepped forward, taking Mac with her. "Yes, can I bring Mac with me? Brooke means a lot to him."

The nurse glanced over to Mac.

Please don't let her say no.

"Of course, but only for a moment. We'll be moving Ms Fairfax to ICU shortly."

Mac followed Louise through the doors, past a circular desk in the middle of the unit, to a cubical where Brooke lay pale and quiet. She had her forehead bandaged and an IV drip attached to her hand. Nasal cannulas wrapped around her head, giving her oxygen. A heart monitor measured the rate of her heart beats.

He and Louise stood either side of the bed looking down at the person they loved. Mac gathered

Brooke's slim hand in his and raised it to his lips. He fought to keep himself under control. If he lost his composure now, he'd be of no use to Brooke or Louise.

"Come back to us, princess," he whispered, kissing her temple.

The same nurse who had ushered them into the ED came towards them. "You'll have to leave now. We're ready to move Ms Fairfax."

Mac wanted to tell her to go to hell, but allowed her to move him away from Brooke's bed.

"Where is ICU?" Louise asked.

"Take the elevator to the third floor. It's directly opposite when you get out. Someone will come out once Ms Fairfax is settled."

"Thank you," Louise replied.

Louise clutched Mac's hands gently. "She'll be all right. She's like my father, very strong-willed."

"Do you think that's enough?"

"I have to."

Fred and Beth came to them as soon as they re-entered the waiting room.

"How is she, lad?" Beth asked.

"They're moving her to ICU, so they must believe she is going to be okay, or they would have had her in the helicopter to Newcastle by now," Mac said. "Monty warned me on the way here what could happen."

"Yes, well that's a good sign," Fred replied.

"Why don't you and Beth go home?" Mac said.

"There's no telling how long we'll be here. I'll call as soon as we know anything."

Fred and Beth exchanged a glance as if they were going to argue the point, but Beth said, "Okay, lad. As soon as you know something, promise you'll ring."

"I promise."

His friends left, leaving Louise and Mac staring, still holding hands until the doors closed.

They took the lift up to ICU and waited. Louise kept his mind busy, talking about Davey and his desire to play soccer with his friends.

"Brooke and I'll make sure we go to every game," Mac said.

Half an hour later they were shown into Brooke's room in ICU. It was a glassed area with only a bed and medical equipment, leaving enough room that if the patient needed to be attended to quickly, there was no congestion. A nurse sat at the end of the bed behind a raised desk so she could observe her patient better. Each patient had one nurse to look after them. Two chairs were brought in for Mac and Louise, and they settled in, waiting for Brooke to open her eyes.

Mac held her hand, not wanting to let go, hoping that while they were connected she would wake up. Louise sat on the other side of the bed, brushing her hand over Brooke's hair.

"Do you know she is the image of a young Ruth? That was one of the reasons my dad was so close to Brooke."

Mac raised an eyebrow. "One of the reasons?"

Louise smiled. "You've been around Brooke. You know how deeply she cares about people. Not just family, but anyone she knows. Dad was like that. They had that connection."

They fell into silence, each caught in their own thoughts of the woman who lay between them. Mac lifted Brooke's hand to his lips.

"Come back to me, princess. My life is empty without you." He didn't care that Louise was in the room with them, he just needed Brooke to know he loved and needed her more than life itself. "I love you, Brooke, you are all I want. Please come back to us. Your mum is here with me, Davey is at home waiting for you. Please fight the fog you are in, please come back to us." He stopped as tears and raw pain broke through his defences. A tear dropped onto their joined hands.

***

Brooke could hear the words drawing her back from the darkness. Mac's voice telling her he loved her, her mother and Davey needing her. She opened her eyes slightly, bright lights blinded her and for a moment, she wanted to return to the darkness.

"Come back, princess. I love you."

Her hand felt as if it was enclosed in a warm glove. Silence fell. *Don't stop. Don't stop talking.*

Something wet fell on her hand. A tear, Mac's tear. She didn't know how, but she knew it was Mac crying for her, calling her back. Her head hurt. *What had happened?*

A crash, there was a crash. A crash then her car had gone into a spin.

"Princess, can you hear me? Fight your way back. Come back to me."

She fought against the light again. Her eyes fluttered. She squeezed the hand holding hers, wanting Mac to know she could hear him.

A shadow fell between her and the light. "You can do it, princess, fight."

She opened her eyes and saw Mac standing over her, his deep blue eyes full of tears, a brilliant smile across those full lips she wanted to taste this very moment.

"Oh, thank God you're back." He pressed his lips to hers, a shadow of a kiss, nothing like they'd experienced before, but it told her so much more of the depth of his love. He moved and she turned to see her mother's tears running down her pale cheeks.

"Mum," she whispered.

"Darling, it is so good to see you awake." Her mother gave a relieved smile.

"Let me have a look at her," a softly accented voice said.

Mac let go of her hand. She wanted him back.

"I'm not going anywhere, I'll be right here."

She held eye contact with him. She nodded, but her head hurt. She lifted her hand to the bandage on her head.

"You took a good bump to your head, but you'll be fine now. Rest will help you recover sooner." The nurse patted her arm and left.

Mac returned and picked up her hand from the bed, pressing his lips to each finger.

Brooke sighed, "I love you, Mac," as she drifted back to sleep.

***

In the two days since Brooke was moved to a regular ward, Mac had only left her side once when her mother and Tyrelle brought Davey for a visit. Her brother was very impressed with the bandage on her head.

"Elle, you bandage Davey's head like Roo's?"

"Sure, bud. We can do that when we get home."

"Elle took Davey fishing, Roo, at the river."

Brooke loved having her family with her, but missed Mac. He returned with a spring in his step and in somewhat of a teasing mood. His smile brightened every time he glanced her way giving her a wink. He was acting very mysterious, and Brooke wasn't sure she liked it. He was hiding something. She could feel it in her bones.

At night, he lay on the bed with her until one of the nurses came around and suggested the chair. He often crept back onto the bed later in the night where he'd kiss her deeply and continually tell her how much he loved her.

On the morning of the third day, her mother walked in with a bright smile on her now relaxed face. "Darling, it will be so good to have you home. Davey constantly asked last night why you couldn't come home yesterday."

"I'll be glad to get out of here as well, Mum. We're all ready, discharge papers signed."

Mac pushed her in the wheelchair that she had been informed she must stay in until she left the hospital.

Her mother opened the front passenger door. Then as Brooke stood, Mac gathered her into his arms and deposited her gently on the seat.

"I could have walked, you know?" But she was smiling. She thrilled at the feel of his arms across her back and under her legs.

He kissed the tip of her nose. "I know, princess, but I like you in my arms." His intense eyes made her body tingle like it was on fire.

"You drive, Mac," her mother said with an amused smirk on her lips.

Brooke blushed.

Once back at Ingalls Estate, Mac lifted her from the car again and carried her into the house. He sat her on one of the overstuffed sofas in the sitting room and kissed her nose.

"Roo, home!" Davey's excited voice rose from the landing above.

"Slow down, Davey, or you'll fall," Tyrelle's voice was followed by the sound of footsteps on the stairs.

Davey ran into the room, his eyes like saucers. He went to jump on Brooke, but Mac stepped in to lift him off his feet.

"You have to slow down, buddy. Brooke had an

accident, remember? And you don't want to hurt her, do you?"

Davey shook his head and lowered his eyes. "Davey naughty."

Brooke's heart broke when Mac placed a finger under Davey's chin so they could look into each other's eyes.

"No, you weren't naughty, buddy, just over-excited to see Brooke home. I have never met a little boy who is as good as you." He pressed his lips to her brother's forehead.

Brooke glanced at her mother and Tyrelle, and saw them both in tears as well. *He is going to be such a good father.* They hadn't talked about marriage, but Brooke hoped they would do so soon.

Mac placed Davey on the seat beside Brooke, and she wrapped an arm around his shoulders, cuddling him into her side.

"I've missed you, little man."

She received a big toothless grin. "Davey miss Roo." He eased up onto his knees to hug her.

Mathew and Ellen bustled into the room carrying trays with tea, coffee and plates of cakes. Brooke looked up to see Mac walking back down the hall with Ruth holding onto his arm.

"Gran Ruth, we have a party," Davey said enthusiastically. "Roo home."

"So she is, darling."

Davey had accepted Ruth as part of the family as if she had been with them forever. He never made a comment that their father was no longer around.

Candice arrived, her face ashen and eyes red. She hesitated at the door before coming in to sit by her mother.

"Do you know who was driving the other car?" Tears gathered in her sister's eyes.

"It was some young kid out for a run in his father's new car," Mac replied. "He and his parents came to visit Brooke at the hospital and apologised. I don't think he will be doing anything so stupid again. I'll see Fred about putting the kid to work at the garage."

"So it wasn't—"

"No." Brooke patted the seat, encouraging her sister to sit by her. If they were going to have a new start, this would be a great time to kick things off.

***

Mac was anxious for the morning tea to be over so he could have time alone with Brooke. She had become the centre of his world these past few days, and it was time for them to make some definite plans. He kept a close eye on Brooke waiting for any signs that things might be getting too much for her. She rested her head back against the sofa and closed her eyes.

"I think it's time I take Brooke up to her bed," he blurted out.

"I can—"

He lifted her in his arms again. "No, I'll carry you."

With goodbyes and sleep wells following them up the stairs, Mac inhaled the subtle aroma of Brooke that washed over him, making him want to hold her in his arms forever.

Brooke's bedcovers had been folded back to reveal crisp white sheets. Mac sat on the bed with her on his lap.

"I've wanted to do this all morning," he said then brushed his lips over hers.

He broke the kiss, running his gaze over her face to her hair. The bandage had been removed from her head and replaced with gauze. "Come on, let's get you into bed." He shifted her to the bed then lifted her feet onto his lap and removed her ugg boots, rubbing each foot as he did.

"You have beautiful feet." Her choke of laughter caused him to raise his head. "What? I can't comment on your feet?"

***

Brooke held her breath as she gazed into Mac's eyes. There was something more than passion within their depths. He kissed her again softly then left her and walked to her dressing table before returning with a small timber box Her heartbeat escalated, hammering against her chest. He knelt before her, taking her left hand in his much larger hands.

"Brooke Angelia Rose Fairfax, would you do me the honour of becoming my wife, my lover, my best friend and my soul mate for now and forever? I love you more than I will ever be able to tell you."

Tears ran down her cheeks. This was everything she had dreamed her life to be, to have a man who truly loved her for who she was and not for what they could get from her.

"I love you too, Mac. You are my heart, but you have to know that if you marry me, you take on Davey as well."

His smile told her all she needed to know even before he answered. "I wouldn't expect anything else."

"Then I would be honoured to be your wife, your best friend, your soul mate and your lover."

He slipped the solitaire diamond ring on her finger then kissed it, before taking her in his arms. He framed her face with his hands and kissed her tenderly. Brooke wound her arms around his neck and pulled him down onto the bed with her then pushed her body closer to his hard form. A low groan escaped from Mac as he deepened the kiss. Their tongues danced the slow sensual dance of lovers. His ran his hands down over her ribs to her waist, pulling her closer. He smelled fresh, like air and spice. Her breath caught as he cupped one breast in his hands. Her nipple beaded.

When he removed his mouth, her lips felt bare. She moaned when he held them a whisper away. "I want nothing more than to make love to you at this moment, but I'm afraid that pleasure will have to wait for us, princess."

Brooke grinned. "That's what you think," she whispered, and kissed him.

~ THE END ~

A little about the Bindarra Creek Romance series: 13 months. 13 authors. 13 romances.

Welcome to Bindarra Creek, a struggling country town where people work hard and love deeply. Set in the picturesque tablelands of New England, Australia, Bindarra Creek is a fictional, drought stricken community full of intrigue, adventure, drama and romance.

Life and love in a small country town has never been more challenging.

Books in the Bindarra Creek Romance series:

Bindarra Creek Makeover - S. E. Gilchrist

Shadows of the Heart - Lee Christine

Second Chance Love - Susanne Bellamy

The CEO Mechanic - Sandie James

Reach for the Stars - Kerrie Paterson

Home to Bindarra Creek - Juanita Kees

Stolen Sanctuary - Stacey Nash

Tempting Fate - Erin Moira O'Hara

One More Day - Linda Charles

The Vine - Lauren McKellar

The Ghost of His Past - Simone Angela

Joanie's Dilemma - Marianne Theresa

Buckley's Chance - Noelle Clark

For more info on the other stories in this series, please visit

www.bindarracreekromance.com

ABOUT THE AUTHOR

At the age of fifteen, I picked up my first Mills and Boon novel and fell in love with the heroes and heroines and their struggle to find happiness. Then I read Jane Austen's Pride and Prejudice and was lost in the world of Historical Romance, never thinking that one day I would find myself writing stories of long ago heroes and heroines.

I love living in Australia with its diversity of beauty from the ocean coastlines to the dryness of the outback. My contemporary romances will take you on a ride across the length and breadth of our beautiful country, the place I call home.

My love of history started from an early age, when my Dad would tell me the stories of our ancestors coming to Australia from England, one side as free settlers, other side as convicts.

My historical stories will transport you through the Georgian and Regency Eras, with strong heroes and heroines determined to live their lives the way they choose not how society dictates.

Links:

You can find more about me by visiting me on line via my website.

www.sandiejames.com

Follow me on Facebook
https://www.facebook.com/sandiejames57

Twitter Handle ~ @sandiejames54

Coming in 2016

Logans Run Series

Return to Hampton Park
In Love With a Cowboy